LIBERTY

ALSO BY ANDREA PORTES

ANATOMY OF A MISFIT

THE FALL OF BUTTERFLIES

LIBERTY

Andrea Portes

An Imprint of HarperCollinsPublishers

HarperTeen is an imprint of HarperCollins Publishers.

Library of Congress Control Number: 2017932853

ISBN 978-0-06-242199-9
ISBN 978-0-06-267332-9 (intl ed)

Typography by Ellice M. Lee
17 18 19 20 21 PC/LSCH 10 9 8 7 6 5 4 3 2 1
❖
First Edition

FOR MY MOM AND DAD,
you will always be my bedrock.
FOR MY HUSBAND,
you will always be my hearth.
FOR MY SON,
you will always be my sky.

PRELUDE

Everything comes to you in dust and waves. The light, the sand blowing in from the crack in the car door, just enough to pass in front of my mother. A two-dimensional face with my father beside her. Halfway across the world. He's saying something about getting ready—Hey, honey, get ready, we're almost there. Something about a checkpoint. I hear my voice coming through the screen: What are you doing there, Mom, what are you even doing there?

She tries to be kind, tries to be understanding. Now, the words are all nothing to worry about—please don't be upset, we'll be home soon.

My voice says, What could be so important, what could be so

goddamn important to force you out of Istanbul, and farther up the road to God knows where?

Damascus, she says. And it's safe and there's a mission there and the nuns won't leave, in spite of the danger. And this is what we do, honey, this is what we do.

Then my father says something about Here we are, here we are at the checkpoint. The driver is speaking to my father, in Arabic, my father answers, and for a moment everything is routine, just papers and IDs a few questions and even a little joke about the ID picture—I was younger then, boy, was I.

I'm about to speak, but my words never get to come out again because then there is gunfire.

Gunfire in bursts and Arabic and dust clouding the air and orders rapid-fire coming from somewhere outside the car and the screen isn't showing my mom anymore, or my dad. The screen is showing the bottom of the backseat of the car while the sound keeps going rat-a-tat-tat, rat-a-tat-tat.

No good-bye words, no kind assurances, not even enough time for I love you.

Only bullets.

"Mom? What's happening? Where are you, tell me now, where are you?!"

But the screen has nothing to say now, and the car has

nothing to say, and there are no more words coming from the car because the car is now empty.

The car is empty.

"Mom? . . . Dad?"

And now there is only silence.

I

1

It's okay for me to tell my story now, isn't it? I mean, there's a couple of things I should probably leave out. Just to make everybody feel better. So as not to shatter our illusions that the world is a wonderful place or whatever.

But maybe there's no point to that. You know, whitewashing. Maybe it's better to just put it all on the table so you can just look at it and decide if you want to see it for what it is, or just unsee it and walk away. I mean, really, it's your choice.

A lot of people unsee a lot of things, every day. Think about it. Every day you go around, stepping over some guy out on the street, outside the Starbucks, or at the park, or on the sidewalk, you just unsee it. Or those cops pulling over that black guy or that brown guy or that anything-but-white guy. You just kind of unsee it, right?

And then, one day, you just kind of forget you're even unseeing anything at all. It's just subconscious. It's just white noise. It's just normal.

But then, sometimes, a person comes along, or a thing comes along, and it jars you. It snaps you out of it. And all of a sudden you can see again.

That's when you have to make the choice.

Am I gonna go back? Or am I gonna keep seeing that?

Because if I keep seeing that, that thing right in front of me that is so unjust, eventually I might have to do something about it.

Look, I'm not here to change anyone's life or anything. I'm just trying to tell a story. But I'm asking . . . what I'm asking is . . . Can I just tell it? Can I just tell it how it happened?

If I tell it to you, you have to keep it safe, okay?

Just keep it safe.

2

All right, well, obviously there's some details we have to go over. You're probably gonna want to know who this right here is. You know, yours truly. The one invading your life right now.

I'm an expat. Well, I'm not really an expat. I'm more the child of two expats. So, therefore, my expat status was forced on me.

Don't worry. I'm not mad at them about it. I couldn't be mad at them even if I wanted to be.

They're dead.

Or *probably* dead.

No one knows.

We're going to get to that later. And don't feel sorry for

me. I can't stand it when I tell people because the look of concern alone is enough to make me want to run out of the room to the nearest bar. Seriously.

Also, just, do me a favor. When I tell you what happened . . . don't freak out.

The whole thing started with something stupid. I mean, really banal.

It's always something stupid. Something you never thought would amount to anything. Something you didn't even think about. In movies you always know when *the big thing* is happening. The music swells. The camera swoops in. The star looks up in wonder. And you know. This is *the big thing*. The life-changing thing.

But not in life. In life it's just a shrug and I did this thing, and then that thing happened, and then this happened. And you never know what the big thing is until you look back and think, OMG, that was it. How did I not know it?

It's maddening in a way. How random it is.

Like this thing. This life-changing thing.

Wanna know what it is?

Applebee's.

Yup, Applebee's.

More specifically, the Applebee's off Interstate 99 just outside of Altoona. That is Pennsylvania, just in case for some reason you didn't know where ALTOONA is. This is the place that fate set me down one happy, unknowing spring day in April 2015. I was driving back from Pittsburgh, listening to Majical Cloudz, minding my own business, when, quite simply, nature called. Nature called and I had to make a stop in this godforsaken place, which, let's be honest, is in the middle of the Appalachian Mountains. That's right. *Deliverance* city. And the only place open that looked like I would not get kidnapped and put in a cellar, the entrance to which is disguised by an icebox, was the Altoona Applebee's of Logan Valley Mall. (Proudly serving a happy hour special of Sweet Chili Brisket Sliders!) Normal, right? But make no mistake, if I hadn't gone to the Applebee's off Interstate 99, two hours outside of Pittsburgh, none of this would have ever happened.

Now, what was I doing in Pittsburgh? Well, my parents raised me to be kind of a knee-jerk liberal—you know, one of those people who annoys everybody at the dinner table by talking about polar bears dying off or #blacklivesmatter and actually caring about sea slaves off the coast of Asia? Yup. I'm one of those. An agitator.

My folks didn't do this because they wanted to annoy everyone around me for the rest of their lives. They didn't even do it on purpose. I could have become a red-faced Tea Party hysteric for all they cared, because the decision was left to me because they are/were namby-pamby liberals who believe this crazy thing that everyone gets to be whatever they want.

But they are/were journalists. And good ones. They had a little flirty competition between them about who had the most Robert F. Kennedy awards, and who got in the *New York Times* and who could possibly get the National Book Award. (My mom did, four years ago, and I think she wore it as a hat for two months straight.)

But let's not talk about them right now, because I don't want to start crying yet. I just want to tell you why I was in Pittsburgh in the first place.

There's a place in Pittsburgh called Carnegie Mellon University where they have an award-winning program in robotics. Without getting into what they are designing there and scaring the bejesus out of you, I will just say, I wanted to see it myself, take notes, talk to the designers, and write about it for my senior thesis on artificial intelligence. So far, the working title is: "Artificial Intelligence: Human Immortality or Frankenstein's Monster?" Look, we can talk about it later.

The problem is, I am still a human with human functions, and that means I had to visit a human bathroom in a human restaurant called Applebee's.

It was supposed to be easy. It was supposed to be a quick stop. Simple.

The thing is . . . there were a lot of families there. Cute families. Families with little kids drawing with crayons on those little paper place mats they give to make kids stay at the table and not run around all over the place tripping waitresses. There were babies, and toddlers, and five-year-old boys in Batman shirts. There was even a little girl dressed as Elsa. For no reason. It's not Halloween. But go ahead, cutie pie, you dress up as Elsa all you want. You do *you*.

And that would have been great, the families.

Except that when you came out of the bathroom, if you looked at the faces of the mommies, you would see something was wrong. Something was really wrong. The moms were worried. The moms were freaking out but trying not to freak out because they were in front of their kids, and all moms know you have to keep it together in front of your kids or they will be terrified.

So I look. I go to see why they are worried. I can't help but feel bad for them. Moms have it hard enough. *You* try taking care of kids. I babysat once and had to take a nap for a week.

And then I see it. Or more aptly, I see *them*.

These guys.

Two of them.

We'll call them Hot Dog and Hamburger. Why will we call them Hot Dog and Hamburger? Because one is tall and weighs three pounds and the other is short and weighs about three hundred. But that's not what's wrong with them. Don't be a jerk.

What's wrong with them is this:

These guys are both just standing there. One in a Confederate flag jean jacket. One in a Slayer shirt. They seem to have matching mullets. They seem to have cut them themselves. But, again, that's not what's wrong with them. Don't be superficial.

What's wrong with them is that they are both carrying what appear to be assault rifles, AK-47s, strapped to their backs, just flung over their backs, like they are in the Applebee's in Iraq. (Which doesn't exist.) They both have extra, just-in-case guns in their holsters as well. Handguns.

If you spoke to them, I bet they would tell you that they are very proud of their guns. They are in LOVE with their guns! They want to marry their guns! But you won't have time to speak with them.

Right now they are harassing the poor manager of the Applebee's, who kind of looks like a much younger Ned Flanders from *The Simpsons*. Here's the conversation:

"Sir, I'm going to have to ask you to leave; there are families here, and you are disturbing their meals."

The moms look worried. Everyone is leaning in. One mom is leaving, huddled over her kids on the way out. I don't blame her. Most of the other moms are anxiously look-ing for their waiters, wanting to leave. There don't seem to be any dads here today. Maybe they are all at work. It is eleven a.m. on a Tuesday, after all.

Hot Dog and Hamburger reply with a card. It looks to be some laminated thing. I peer over their shoulders. Oh, a copy of the Constitution. Of course!

Hamburger takes the lead: "It is my God-given right to be here. It is my right to be armed. This is a free country the last time I checked."

Hot Dog chimes in: "Yeah, our forefathers got it for us!"

I'm sure Thomas Jefferson would be thrilled.

More moms leave, panicked.

And I can't help it.

This is something I shouldn't do but I do anyway.

(I've never been very good at social norms.)

I step in.

"Good afternoon, Hot Dog and Hamburger! I believe it's time you leave this establishment!"

3

I think I forgot to tell you that I'm five foot two and have mouse-brown hair and skin the color halfway between paper and the inside of a potato. Also, I'm a bit underweight because I have what the doctor's have informed us is called "dissociative disorder," which makes me not realize that I actually have a body and that I'm actually supposed to feed said body.

So I'm not exactly big. And I'm not exactly tough-looking. And I'm in the middle of the Appalachian Mountains.

So you can imagine the look they give me.

It's not quite laughter.

It's more incredulousness.

It's more . . . *What the eff does this little elf think she's doing here?*

It's more . . . *Are you kidding me, tiny?*

And they're all staring now. The mothers. The waiters. Even the little ones. Those little baby faces, rapt. And I have to protect them. I don't know *why* I feel like it's my job. But for some reason, it is.

And somehow it seems this is not really happening. That the moment I spoke up I stepped into an alternate universe.

"Are you fucking kidding?" It's Hamburger. He's the leader.

"Gentlemen, and I use the term loosely, I would like you to refrain from using profanity in front of the children. Many of them are not yet five and should not be submitted to hearing such vulgarity. However, the more pressing issue *is that I would like you to leave this establishment.*"

"You high or something?" That was Hot Dog. He's obviously the brains of the operation.

"I will give you to the count of three."

Now Hamburger.

"I will give YOU til the count of three, sweet cheeks. How 'bout that?"

He pulls out his handgun. Aims it at me.

Welp, that escalated quickly.

I turn to Ned, the manager. "You see this, right? Assault with a deadly weapon?"

Ned just gulps. I turn back to the barbecue twins.

"The sweetness of my cheeks is of no concern to you. Also, the problem is that I have a dissociative disorder. So when you are pointing that gun at me? It's as if you are pointing it at a stranger. Do you understand?"

They don't really know what to make of this.

Who would know what to make of it? Imagine if you see yourself from outside of yourself. Like you are a fly on the ceiling watching yourself. And right now, with a gun pointed at me in the hospitality area of the Applebee's in Altoona, I most definitely feel like I am watching myself.

"I'm going to give you one last chance to leave this establishment."

They stand there.

"Are you sure? I really don't want to humiliate you in front of all these people. Although, truthfully, you have already humiliated yourselves by bringing a semiautomatic weapon to the Applebee's."

"Shut the hell up, stupid bitch."

The gun, still pointed, not two feet away.

"I see. So you insist upon the swearing. Again, I'm a pacifist at heart, so—"

"Yeah, suck it, hippie."

"Let's count it down, shall we? ONE . . ."

The manager and the waitresses look at each other and sink down behind the host's stand.

"TWO . . ."

The moms shelter their kids, moving them back toward the tables.

"TWO AND A HALF."

The guys chuckle now. They think it's ridiculous. They think I'm stalling.

We don't get to three.

If Hamburger knew what he was doing, he would not be pointing his gun that close. Because that is just close enough for me to reach out, grab his gun, twist his hand back, and point the gun right back at him. Using the ancient Filipino marshall art of Eskrima. Which he doesn't know. And obviously he doesn't know that I know.

And, let's face it, you didn't know I knew it either. It's not something I go around bragging about. That would just be lame. But, suffice to say, my mom became kind of obsessed with Muay Thai, Eskrima, jujitsu, and good old-fashioned karate while I was growing up. So that meant we all had to be obsessed, too.

It's not their fault. Hot Dog and Hamburger.

I don't exactly look like a black belt.

Hot Dog tries to grab me from behind, but that is actually

the perfect positioning for me to flip him over my back and send him crashing to the floor. I mean, like, that's literally where they have your sparring partner stand to practice that move on the mat.

THUD.

And there goes his AK-47. Which now falls to the floor and, praise the Lord, doesn't discharge. I grab that particular health hazard just in time to see Hamburger charge me with the full weight of his flame-grilled burger body. Which would be daunting. Absolutely. Except if you use the force of his endless life of funnel cakes against him and simply wait until the very last moment before stepping aside in a lightning-quick manner, then he ends up using all of his own weight to run barreling into the bubblegum machine.

Kind of humiliating.

If these guys weren't such dicks I'd feel sorry for them. But let's remember who brought the AK-47s to the Applebee's, now, shall we?

Hamburger's face is bleeding, lacerated by the gum-ball dispenser. Also, his nose looks pretty bad. Not that it looked that good before. This is a great time to grab *his* AK, which, let's be honest, is not going to go well with his oncoming blind rage. I notice Hot Dog get up from the ground because his reflection is actually visible in the glass of the gum-ball machine. He is currently coming up behind me.

See? If I wasn't seeing this from the ceiling, I might actually be terrified right now.

The thing about guns is that you can always use the butt of them. Which I do. And now he's smacked to the ground bleeding, too. Hamburger seems to still be in a state of shock. Hot Dog is cursing to himself. Both of them are kind of just flailing around there on the floor of the Applebee's welcome area.

So *that* happened.

The waitstaff, the manager, the moms look at me. Like I am from Pluto.

They did not see it coming.

It's a five-year-old who breaks the silence, the one in the Batman shirt.

"Did you see that, Mommy?! That was awesome!"

And his mom allows herself a kind of relieved laugh.

I remove the ammunition from both guns, then hand the guns and ammo, separately, to Ned Flanders.

"Okay, well, thank you for the facilities," I say. "By the way, you may want to install a hand air dryer, as it will prove to be an effective cost-cutting measure, as well as reducing paper towel consumption. Something to think about."

I step over Hot Dog and Hamburger. Flick their laminated

Constitution, which I've picked up from the ground, into their faces. "I'm sure you've made George Washington very proud today."

And that's all she wrote. I walk out, leaving the Applebee's of Altoona, Pennsylvania, behind me.

I'm sure it feels like a bit of a daydream to those people in there. But that's okay, too, because, as you know, it all feels like a daydream to me. That's my problem. Or my "crisis/opportunity" as my mom would say.

But, regardless of that, I had to do something.

You see, I hate guns.

And the only thing I hate more than guns is guns around little kids.

I feel passionately about this subject for probably the same reason I have this dissociative disorder. It all goes back to the same part of the brain, which is apparently highly invested in daydreaming, obsession, and, of course, worst-case-scenario *plotting*, otherwise known as worrying. It's the same part. You see, there's no such thing as a free lunch.

But the important thing here, right now? Well, the important thing is I didn't know there was video being shot of the entire incident. I had no idea. And I certainly didn't know that this video would alter the course of the rest of my life.

4

Everyone thinks they're dead.

My parents.

I mean, they try to be nice about it and offer kind words and support. They tell me to have hope. They tell me miracles can happen. Stuff like that. Nothing about rainbows and buttercups just yet. But I'm pretty sure it's coming. I mean, it's been over a year. So the keep-hope-alive speeches are becoming less and less convincing. Particularly to the ones saying them.

If they just would've stopped caring about people, none of this would have happened. If they just would've become like the rest of everybody and never seen the bad stuff, never looked at the bad stuff, just gotten back to the TV and the internet and the infinite distraction, well . . . then they'd probably be safe and sound. Ensconced in a cocoon of their own making.

But no. Not them.

They happened to be in Istanbul for their publisher. Yep, they both had the same publisher in Turkey. It turns out, Turkish people read a lot! There was a big hullabaloo book fair in Istanbul, and their publisher flew them out to sign their respective books and make appearances on local talk shows and the like.

Yep, I know. They're sort of famous. Well, *renowned*. Intellectuals are never really famous. My mom is *renowned* for a book she wrote on multinational corporations, where she actually went undercover and worked at a factory in Bangladesh for ten cents a day. That's the one that got her that National Book Award she's so proud of. Or used to be proud of. Right now she's probably not proud so much because she's probably dead.

Ouch.

I know.

But let's just face facts, shall we?

And my dad. His book, *River to Sea*, taught on campuses from Princeton to Berkeley, has somehow ended up being the seminal book on Israel/Palestine. That got him a National Book Critics Circle nomination. (But not a win.

That year the nonfiction went to *The Warmth of Other Suns* by Isabel Wilkerson. Stiff competition.)

But, in Istanbul? At the Istanbul Book Fair? My parents were rock stars.

That would've been fine. Perfect. All well and good.

Except.

My mom met a woman who was worried about her sister. In Syria. Her sister was a nun at the Catholic Mission northeast of Damascus, halfway to Aleppo. Instead of fleeing the inevitable advance of ISIS, the priest and the nuns decided to stay there, with their flock. Even though most of the people in the town were Muslims. The idea was that it was wrong to abandon the people. That it was their moral duty, their God-given duty, to stay.

So of course my mother wanted to interview them. This noble cause. This nun, this priest, this flock.

She assured my father she'd be safe, but he insisted on joining her. They wouldn't go farther than Damascus.

Damascus, no surprise, is the last place they were seen.

I go over this again and again, each night, tossing and turning, trying to find a clue, somewhere in the plan. A missing piece. Maybe the woman she met at the book fair was a plant. Maybe it was a trap. Where was this Catholic Mission? Who were these nuns? Are they still alive? Is anyone still alive? Where are my parents?

Are they ever coming home?

Will I ever see my dad's rugged skin? His khaki green epaulet button-down shirts, always with a little notepad in the pocket. His hair all over the place, a mad scientist in chestnut. Will he ever tell me his dumb jokes again? Will he ever call me a sack of potatoes and throw me over this shoulder even though I tell him I'm too old and *oh God, Dad, seriously, stop?*

What about my mom?

There are a million things I think about my mom, and her decision to tell this story in the middle of a war zone. I have processed up to five hundred and thirty-one thoughts on the subject thus far. Only nine hundred ninety-nine thousand, four hundred sixty-nine to go!

But will I ever see her again? Her long dishwater-blond hair, her bizarre mismatched outfits, her Bohemian chic, patterns from Mojave to Mumbai? My mom, with her razor-sharp wit and pithy insights. That's the thing about my mom: she was always the smartest and, yes, the weirdest, one in the room.

At first, people would think she was a dummy. They would. They'd see my dad, a little bit older, and looking it from spending years and years from Gaza to the Golan Heights. They'd see my mom, younger than my dad, and young-*looking*. (She was vain.) Then they'd just assume he was some sort of sugar daddy and she was in it for the free ride. But then . . . then . . . she'd say one or two things in conversation that would inevitably identify her as 1) not stupid and 2) kind of a genius. And she'd do it humbly. Then, at some point someone would refer to her superfamous National Book Award–winning book.

Game, set, and match.

Trust me. I've seen it happen over fifteen times. You can practically tell time by it.

The other thing you can tell time by is my mom's ability to lose anything. And I do mean *anything*. Has she ever asked where her keys are when they're in her hand? Check. Has she ever asked you to help her find her phone, when you are talking to her over the phone? Check. What about asking you where her glasses are when she is wearing them? And check.

I have never in my life met anyone more forgetful or absentminded then my mom. She's like beyond the absentminded professor. She's like the loopy, blind, absentminded professor. Here's an example: she cannot, for the life of her, make toast. Toast. She has tried it ten times and every time, every time . . . the toast ends up black. Oh, she'll cut it into pieces. She'll even cut it into little triangles BEFORE she realizes it's black. Then she'll serve it in front of whoever is the unfortunate receiver of the toast, usually Dad or me. And that's when it happens: She'll see it for the first time.

Through your eyes. In reality. "Oh no!" She will declare. "How did that happen?" And she will mean it. She will truly be baffled.

It got so my dad and I had to hide the toaster.

"Please," my dad would insist. "Stop trying. It's okay. You don't have to prove anything. It's just toast."

She'd reply, "Are you sure it's not a metaphor for my love and my ability to create a happy and loving home?"

"Yes. It is not a metaphor for your love and your ability to create a happy and loving home. You're an incredible journalist, mother, and wife. But, let's face it, toast is not your thing."

"It's not my thing?"

"Nope. You are antitoast."

And he'd smile, and she'd smile back.

That moment.

Little moments like that.

I miss them.

So that was it. He was the chef. And Mom would put together whatever ridiculous fun decorations were in fitting with the theme. Chicken kiev for dinner? Let me show you these Russian dolls! Or a Cinco de Mayo night? I'll find a piñata! Let's make paper flowers! My mom had this goofy yet adorable way of going all in. She'd hang Turkish lanterns. She'd rent a popcorn machine. She'd find a way to project a movie onto a big screen in the backyard. She even once, I'm not kidding, hired a quick-change artist. I know. It was so doofy, but it was, undeniably, hilarious.

That's what I think my dad loved about her.

She was like a light.

He was more kind, more serious, more measured. But she was actually a goofball. Imagine Ruth Gordon in *Harold and Maude*. Oh, you haven't seen it? Go see it right now. Seriously.

. . .

I'm waiting . . .

. . .

Okay, you back? Good. Nice to see you again. So, now that you've seen Ruth Gordon in *Harold and Maude* . . .

That's my mom.

It was like all the terrible things in the world manifested in her into a rebellion against darkness. A defiant exuberance.

And this is what makes me think she's alive. That she has to be alive. That there is no way on earth, no God so cruel, no fate so callous, that it would let this particular spirit perish.

I just can't believe it.

But maybe I am just kidding myself.

Maybe they are both dead.

And maybe I am a fool.

5

All three of my boyfriends are shocked LexCorp is recruiting on campus.

Okay, maybe they're not really my *boyfriends*. More like guys who I see a lot but can't commit to. I know, it's weird to have three.

One day they will each of them marry a sweet girl who says the right things and is liked by their respective parents and they'll move into houses with white picket fences and dogs named Spot.

But that ain't me, babe.

I'm not sure why I'm doing this, this having-three-not-boyfriends thing, other than the fact that while I do not want to deal with ONE person in a RELATIONSHIP, I'm deathly afraid of being alone. When I'm alone, the thoughts come rushing in. When I'm alone, all of the too-horrible things that could have happened, or are happening, to my mom and dad threaten to invade my conscience. That's the first problem.

And the second problem? Remember how we were talking about that little dissociative issue I have? Like, I see myself not from inside myself but from somewhere else? Usually from up above or the corner or something? Well, that kinda takes a toll on the old relationship issue. You know how in movies girls are always superexcited when a guy comes close to them and says something sweet or gives them a hug or gives them flowers? Like every girl out there is just dying to bloom into a beautiful butterfly at the touch, the look, the approval of the nearest cute guy? Well, I sort of ended up being the opposite of that girl. So for instance, if a guy goes to kiss me really fast, I shrink away. It scares me. Or if a guy looks into my eyes and says, "I want to be closer to you." It's like a horror show. Terrifying.

And I didn't want to be this way. I didn't ask to be.

It's just something that ended up happening for a lot of different reasons that maybe we can explore later and then make a PowerPoint presentation about.

(Also, then we can make a PowerPoint presentation about why PowerPoint presentations are boring.)

In any case, there's nothing wrong with any of these three guys. I'm serious. It's me. I've investigated the problem, and the problem is me.

Do you want to meet them?

Okay, fine. But before you do, I have to explain a little bit about the situation around these parts.

Ready?

I go to an all-women's college named Bryn Mawr. It's one of the "Seven Sisters," and the thing everyone always says about it is that Katharine Hepburn went here. The other Seven Sisters are, in no particular order, Wellesley, Mount Holyoke, Vassar (the debutante one), Radcliffe (the Harvard one), Smith (girls in pearls), and Barnard (the one in New York). Bryn Mawr is generally considered the one with the freaks. Also, the most academically challenging. And lesbo central.

Now, there are four colleges associated with Bryn Mawr: Princeton, Swarthmore, UPenn, and Haverford.

Princeton is the official brother school of Bryn Mawr, but it's WAY too square and there is zero interaction. Those are guys who strive to be *bankers*. Gross. You can practically feel them itching to crash the economy.

UPenn is also considered part of the community. We can take classes there, but it's in Philadelphia, which is a twenty-five-minute train ride, so it might as well be in Tibet. Also, those guys are kind of jocky. Again, ew.

Swarthmore is closer, and cooler. We can take classes there, and they can take classes here. In fact, last year, five guys took a class with me in English House called "Poetics and Politics of the Sublime." I know. No one had any idea what that class was about. But those guys could talk a blue streak. One of them even had patches on the elbows of his blazer. Patches!

And, finally, there is Haverford. Very much more involved. There's a blue bus that runs between the two schools and we can live there, they can live here, etc. Except no one really does this because those are all guys who listen to Phish, wear flannel, and play lacrosse, and we are all a bunch of black-clad lesbos who chant, "Death to the Patriarchy!" and spell *woman* with a *y*. *Womyn*. Get it? Because the idea is you don't need a man to spell *woman*. Don't laugh.

I don't really care about the spelling thing, but I have no desire to listen to Phish.

However, every once in a while there is a phenomenon called a "Bryn Man." That is a Haverford guy who doesn't really fit over there and will just decide to live and major at Bryn Mawr. They have to have a pretty thick skin and a very studied self-deprecating way about them to get away with it. But these are the smartest guys. Because these guys still get a lot of action. Pretty clever, huh?

So, now that we've laid the groundwork . . . let's meet our bachelors, shall we?

Okay, here we.

Bachelor number one!

Well, folks, bachelor number one hails from Allentown, Pennsylvania! The only son of a Jewish doctor and a doting mother, he was raised as if he is God's gift to the earth and has a habit of being hilarious, pithy, and biting. Olive-skinned with giant dark eyes, bachelor number one is five foot eleven, skinny, and hoping to be a great filmmaker one day. His hobbies include watching obscure movies and watching obscure movies. Ladies and gentlemen, meet Aaron!

Are you ready for bachelor number two? Okay, then, bachelor number two is from sunny Southern California. Having lost his father at a young age, bachelor number two was raised by his German-American mother. However, his grandfather on his father's side was African-American. The combination of this, with his German blood, somehow made him the most attractive person ever to walk the face of the earth and possibly the universe. Dishwater-blond, short hair; beige, sun-kissed skin; and a truly hunky body have turned this guy into, basically, a living Ken doll. But with brains. Yes, folks, bachelor number two is an international relations major who will probably one day be the ambassador to China. Say hello to Teddy!

And finally, bachelor number three is an international student from (sigh) Paris, France. He is filled with disdain for everything American except for his Levi's and Marlboro cigarettes. He wears vaguely Middle Eastern scarves and is a philosophy major whose personal philosophy is *look good, hate everything*. He has the same five-o'clock shadow at all times, although I don't quite know how that's physically possible. His name is . . . Patrice!

So there, now you've met all three of them.

I can't tell if you are impressed or concerned.

Don't worry, they all know about one another. Scout's honor. Or, at least, they each know they are not my one and only. And I'm pretty sure they don't care.

(For the record, I'm sure I'm not their one and only either, although I haven't really bothered to ask.)

There is one thing they do all have in common. At one point or another, all three of them mentioned how baffled, annoyed, or irate they were that LexCorp is coming to our bicollege community to recruit.

Who is LexCorp? Funny you should ask.

LexCorp is probably the least understood and most diabolical company known to man. They make Halliburton look like Bambi. Rumor has it, the company profited by over eighty billion dollars from the Iraq War. Basically, on oil. And retrieving the oil. And overcharging the government to hire its own special workers to drill the oil. And selling the oil. Originally, they were strictly an oil company. Then they decided to branch out into coal, natural gas, and every fossil fuel known to man. But that's not all.

Fun fact: You know those guys who always go on the news to represent the "doubt" over climate change? The ones who say things like "The science isn't in" and "Global warming is a hoax"? Well, those are actually just a small handful of guys. They're called "experts." They always have something under their name implying they are from some obscure "foundation" or "institute."

But, if you actually take the time to look into these so-called foundations and institutes, they are usually shells for the fossil fuel industry. Like, say, LexCorp. So, basically, LexCorp has paid millions and millions of dollars to get these guys on all the news shows, since the 1970s, to make everyone doubt the reality of climate change, thereby dooming us all. Fun fact number two: Many of these guys are the exact same guys who said smoking wasn't bad for you. Nice bunch.

Don't believe me? Look these guys up. Or watch *Merchants of Doubt*. Go ahead. I'll wait.

Whistle, whistle, whistle . . .

. . .

Okay, did you see it? Great.

So now you know I'm not just an insane person with paranoid delusions, and now you also know that we are stuck dealing with the coming onslaught of a warming planet compliments of LexCorp.

I even have a T-shirt that says "LexCorp: We're making a killing!" in 1950s supercheesy ad design. Kind of like the font from an old postcard. You'd really like it. I'll get you one if you're nice to me.

Here's something funny. LexCorp is conducting interviews here at Bryn Mawr from the suicide room. They don't know it's the suicide room. They think it's just the Vandevoort Room. Because that's what it says on the plaque. But what they don't know is that fifty years ago, Tisley Vandevoort, heiress and debutante, committed suicide in that very room. It was all over the society pages. A real scandal. Her family, traumatized, dedicated this gorgeous, elegant room in Denbigh Hall to her. The idea being, I think, to give the students at Bryn Mawr a place to go and relax, muse, and meditate instead of killing themselves. What LexCorp didn't realize is that no one at Bryn Mawr would ever, ever, go into that room. Because, suicide.

The fact that LexCorp is now recruiting from the infamous suicide room suggests to me that someone on the job fair organization committee has a sense of humor.

I bet this was their little rebellion against having to pencil in these guys in the first place. Nicely played, for sure. But LexCorp can't be let off that easily.

I don't know why I think it's my job, but it is. I won't rest until someone calls out the demons from LexCorp on their utter degeneracy.

If you're guessing what I'm doing right now, you're probably right.

I'm walking across the green, through a tree-lined path, from my dorm to Denbigh Hall.

To the suicide room.

To meet with LexCorp.

6

I have to give it to the Vandervoorts. They really knew what they were doing. This is probably the most exquisite room on campus. Persian rugs, mahogany tables with gargoyles carved into the legs, Ming dynasty vases, oil paintings of pastoral scenes involving horses. I mean, these guys knew how to class it up.

At the other side of the room, a pristine seating area. Two wingback chairs in a chinoiserie fabric, navy blue with some kind of birds, facing a navy couch with a complementary navy pattern. There is coral involved in the pattern to make it pop. That's the thing about really fancy places: There's always more humor to it than you see in the movies. A sense of play.

Across the room, sitting in one of the wingback chairs, facing toward the window, there's a man. I can't see his face, but his hair is a kind of dirt brown. And he seems to have all of it.

This is the enemy.

This is the recruiter from LexCorp.

This guy must have some spider sensibilities, because he is up and turning toward me just as I set foot in the room. I didn't even make a noise.

And now he's facing me.

Um . . .

Look, I was expecting this guy to be bald, squat, and weirdly tan in that way that rich guys always seem to be. Trump tan.

But this guy isn't any of those things.

He's actually tall. He's actually pale. And he's actually kind of . . . cool-looking. Like his suit is a sharp, somewhere-between-gray-and-navy thing, with a kind of skinny fit I was not anticipating. And I'm not sure, but there seem to be electrons radiating all around him.

He stops for a second. Stares.

Maybe there are electrons radiating around me?

We both just kind of stand there for an extremely awkward moment.

And then he pulls himself together.

"Paige . . . Nolan? Am I saying that right?"

"Um, yes. It's Nolan. Like Golan. Like the Golan Heights. The place captured from Syria and occupied by Israel during the Six-Day War, territory that Israel effectively annexed in 1981, but which remains a point of contention, *évidemment*."

(That's French for *obviously*.)

He stares at me.

Sometimes this happens to me. Communication with other humans was never my forte.

Now I'm going to share with you the next part of the interview, which consists of a kind of multilingual dance. Don't worry. I'll translate, I promise.

"*Je remarqué que vous parlez français couramment—vous considérez-vous d'être un peu français?*" he throws out there.

Do I *consider myself* part French? That's not what he's really asking, is it? I rapid-fire back *en francais*:

"Either someone is French, or they aren't. You mean, do I scorn everything and hate Americans, as the French do?"

"*Quelque chose comme ça.*" He smiles. *Something like that.*

Smart-ass. He has no idea who he's dealing with. I switch to Russian. "*Pochemu by ne sprosit' menya, yesli ya schitayu sebya svoyego roda russkiy yazyk?*" *Then why not ask me if I consider myself to be kind of Russian?*

"*Prekrasno. Schitayete li vy sebya byt' svoyego roda russkiy?*" *Fine. Do you?*

Huh. So he's trilingual. Color me bored. I switch to a kind of casual Chinese, which I'm sure he won't speak. *"Yěxǔ wǒ rènwéi zìjǐ shì nà zhǒng zhōngguó rén. Zhéxie gongsi de búxié, yînwéi xiǎng nî képå de gongsî zhüyåo shi méiguo."*

Or perhaps I consider myself Chinese. Each of these countries disdains America mainly because of shitty companies like your own.

"Se refiere a nuestra empresa que emplea a cientos de miles de trabajadores en todo el mundo. Mantiene el pan en su mesa."

(He's saying they employ hundreds of thousands of workers across the world. They put bread on their tables.)

"El pan en su mesa! No hay mesa! No hay casa! Hay solamente casa de la cartulina cuadro, por todo la familia!"

(My response. Bread on the table! There is no table! There is no house! There is only a shanty made of cardboard for the whole family! It's only after I'm done that I realize we've switched to Spanish.)

"Algún tipo de Latina? Cuba, tal vez?"

"Yes. Cuban. I learned Spanish from a revolutionary. Uncle Fidel." A joke.

"Touché." He gets it.

We stare at each other. It's not exactly cold. It's more like an assessment and a stalemate.

"Now that that's over with, pleased to meet you. My name's Madden. Carter Madden."

I snort. "Carter. Madden? Are you in a soap opera?"

"Trust me. I wish my parents had named me John or Steve."

He reaches out his hand to shake. Do I shake this man's hand? This LexCorp hand?

I hesitate. He retrieves his hand. Not angrily, exactly. Something else.

"Have a seat."

He gestures toward the seating area, and next thing I know, we are facing each other in our respective wingback chairs. Very fancy.

A normal interview would be behind a desk, I assume. But I suppose they do things slightly differently here at Bryn Mawr.

"So. You're a fan of Sean Raynes?"

"What? How did you know that?"

"He happens to be all over your Twitter feed."

"Um. Why did you check my Twitter feed?"

Let's back up a second and talk about Sean Raynes. Although now people just call him Raynes. He's that famous. And his name is synonymous with whistle-blowing.

Here's what happened.

Raynes was/is a superhacker. Ultrasmart. Top of his class at MIT. Tech genius. Computer whiz. All-around superstar. When he graduates, one year early like I will, he's recruited by the CIA. In tech. Defending against cyberhackers, terrorist attacks, that sort of thing.

And this is all well and good. Until Raynes realizes something horrible is going on and that the horrible thing is not actually coming from cyberhackers.

In fact, he realizes that *the* CIA has put a microchip in EVERY cell phone sold in the United States. The microchip stays dormant. No big deal. Until you, or your mom, or your brother, or your friend, do anything vaguely suspicious. And I do mean *vaguely*. Things like . . . going on vacation to Istanbul, visiting relatives in Cuba, spending a summer in Saint Petersburg. Anything. In that case, you get put on a list. And the chip becomes activated.

Now they can follow you. They can track you. Wherever you go, they know about it.

And this list of "suspected terrorists" should be about ten to twenty thousand people, right? Wrong. The list is over two million names long.

Over two million people tracked, every day, on their cell phones, by the CIA.

Yup.

Big brother is everywhere.

So . . . Sean Raynes discovers this. Sean Raynes has a crisis of conscience.

Sean Raynes knows what the government is doing is wrong; he knows it's a violation of the Constitution and our right to privacy. But he is also a good guy, a patriot, a true believer in America and all it stands for.

So he thinks about it. He ponders and wrings his hands and spends many a sleepless night.

And then he breaks the story on CNN.

To Anderson Cooper, no less.

And while that story was crashing over the television airwaves—breaking, as it were—Raynes, en route to Nepal, was forced to land in Moscow. Where he abides today, in a sort of purgatorial state.

Putin refuses to extradite him, as he is an embarrassment to the US government. And, meanwhile, back in the States, it is becoming more and more clear that this guy is a hero.

Statues are being raised to him, illegally, in places from Williamsburg, Brooklyn, to Echo Park, Los Angeles. In Austin, Texas, they even held a parade in his honor.

But to many other Americans, he is considered a traitor.

Guess which side I'm on.

But let's get back to the classy meeting, shall we?

"I fail to understand why you would be searching my Twitter feed."

Madden feigns interest in my résumé.

"You scheduled an appointment with us. Don't you think it's relevant information?"

"I think the only relevant information is that you work

for a company that has almost single-handedly stalled climate change action for thirty years, dooming all of us to runaway global warming."

Madden looks up.

"I think it's *relevant information* that your company profited billions of dollars off an unjustified war that killed hundreds of thousands of people, many of whom were women and children."

He tilts his head, looks out the window.

"Yes, I am aware of your opinions."

Wait. What?

"Then why did you . . . why are we . . . Were you hoping to convince me otherwise?"

"No, actually. I was just hoping to meet you."

"Excuse me?"

"And now that I have, I'm satisfied. *Arigato gozeimas ta.*"

(That last part is Japanese. Directly translated, it means, "It has all been very good with us." But it's a way of saying a final thank-you. A good-bye.)

And just like that, Madden is out the door.

I am left there.

In the suicide room.

To contemplate what just happened.

No.

No, no, no, no, no. This is not over. LexCorp does *not* get the last word.

I decide to get in touch with this guy's boss. I'm not sure what kind of operation they're running over there, but I'd really like to understand why anyone would be poking into my Twitter feed *before* an interview.

The registrar's office is just across the garden, so it's really no effort to pop in. It's a tiny gray stone building that was the original student hall of Bryn Mawr. Inside, it's dusty, with piles of paper everywhere.

I poke my head in to see the registrar.

"Hello. Sorry to bother you. Do you think it might be possible to get the phone number for whomever your contact is at LexCorp?"

The registrar looks up. She's a redheaded woman with glasses on a chain and a burgundy cardigan.

"Excuse me?"

"Your LexCorp contact. I was wondering if I could get the number?"

"I'm sorry, I'm a bit confused here . . ."

"I just had the strangest interview."

"With who?"

"With LexCorp. They were here, you know, for recruitment?"

She takes off her glasses and stares at me, sizing me up.

"You're joking, right?"

"Why would I be joking?"

"Young lady, LexCorp has been banned from our campus since nineteen seventy-eight."

7

This is the moment I should probably leave campus and never look back.

Because *what the hell was that?*

But of course, that's not what I do.

Instead, I just keep on going about my business, thinking possibly this fake LexCorp interview was just some figment of my imagination, some dumb fluke, nothing to see here.

After all, I have midterms to take, papers to write, books to read. It's not as if I have all the time in the world to contemplate the random appearance of a particularly striking person who knew my name and *feigned an entire corporate interview.* Weird? Yes. A possible threat to my GPA? No. Not a chance.

And the tonic I have, the answer for quelling my thoughts, is surely one of my three not-boyfriends. Any time, day or night, I can text either Aaron from Allentown, Teddy from Santa Monica, or Patrice from Paris. No big deal. No questions. No answers. No one gets hurt.

This random texting happens a lot.

Once the books are closed, once the papers are written, there is that time, the witching hour, when the last thing I want to do is think but all I can do is think, and imagine, and *despair*. Truly despair. Like to the point of being catatonic. Unable to get off the bed. Unable to move. Frozen.

I've pinpointed the moment—that moment before the whole thing falls apart and begins to snowball. And it's in this moment that I've trained myself to text. Just text. Find Aaron. Find Teddy. Find Patrice. The first one to text back is what happens next. Not the abyss. A tonic, instead. A boy to keep my mind off it. A boy to not face facts.

But this particular evening, tonight, I have reached that moment. I have texted, but to no avail. It's eleven p.m. and there is no sign of boy tonic. Anywhere.

There I sit, staring at the wooden slats of the dorm room floor. They're a kind of medium beige. At our old house, in Berkeley, my mom insisted on dark brown floors. A kind of alpine color, associated with cabins. But then the walls were white. It was a kind of stark contrast, which just happened to be perfect. That was always the way it was with my mom. She just threw things together in a way that most people would think was completely bizarre, you'd never think of it, and then you'd look at it all together in the end and it would stun you. Wow, you'd think, how did she do that?

I'm using the past tense again.

To describe my mom.

I have to get out of here.

There's a path, down the hill behind my dorm, leading through the trees and then up the hill to town. It winds, here, at the edges of the campus, across the green and past the duck pond. Now, with the entire campus either asleep or frantically writing papers somewhere behind a dim light, there's the strange sound of nothing. Not even white noise. Or a passing car. In the distance, above the trees, a few flickering lights in the dorm-room windows. The night owls.

I never noticed it before. Here. This inlet. There's a hidden little grove of elms and then, in the back, a small plaque underneath a copper statue. The statue is a man, clasped around his waist by an anchor. But he is facing the other way, against the weight of the anchor, refusing to bend under its weight. The tiny plaque, lit up, in the faintest of lights, a poem:

DO NOT GO GENTLE INTO THAT GOOD NIGHT

Do not go gentle into that good night,
Old age should burn and rave at close of day;
Rage, rage against the dying of the light.
Though wise men at their end know dark is right,
Because their words had forked no lightning they
Do not go gentle into that good night.
Good men, the last wave by, crying how bright
Their frail deeds might have danced in a green bay,
Rage, rage against the dying of the light.
Wild men who caught and sang the sun in flight,
And learn, too late, they grieved it on its way,
Do not go gentle into that good night.
Grave men, near death, who see with blinding sight
Blind eyes could blaze like meteors and be gay,
Rage, rage against the dying of the light.
And you, my father, there on the sad height,
Curse, bless, me now with your fierce tears, I pray.
Do not go gentle into that good night.
Rage, rage against the dying of the light.
—Dylan Thomas

I stand there for a lost amount of time, transfixed by this
night message. This missive. It seems, in the pitch black,

in this lonely patch of grass, that this was somehow meant for me. Just me. A turning to this unmapped place for no reason. I look around me. Of course, there's no one. Just me and the secret statue. Is it here at all?

I stay here for a spell, stare at the sky. Nope. No answer there.

Just these words and this moment.

I take a few steps backward, still in cahoots with the statue, before stepping out back onto the path. This path winds its way into town, away from groves of quiet contemplation and toward raucous obliteration. Toward forgetting.

In town, there's a row of bars—the Night Owl, Footsies, the Gold Room, the Lamplighter, the Short Stop—the kind of bars with red benches, lots of locals, regulars, and college kids mixed in. Sometimes even a drunken brawl. Townies vs college kids. The townies usually win.

Ten blocks farther, solemn and staid, a converted Tudor estate, a hotel on the hill, hidden by the foliage, little dark lanterns through the leaves.

Before I know it, I'm on that path. On that path, past the bars. Definitely not going into any of those bars. Last thing I want is to see someone from school. Or, worse, to see one of my nonboyfriends with some girl. That would be depressing. Or, at least, awkward.

No, the hidden hotel it is.

This place is called the Tillington.

Established in 1863.

I guess it's called the Tillington because that was the original family, the original estate. Who knows where they are now, but they sure left behind a nice place.

It's kind of an old standby for me. The place is Tudor, so everything is kind of dark and brown inside. There's candles everywhere, so you could really spook out here. There's a formal white-tablecloth dining room *avec* fireplace and dark wood rafters above. There's a casual bistro for sandwiches. And an atrium brunch room with giant windows and cherry blossoms all around. Very romantic. But right now all of those places are closed. Nope. The only thing open is that hovel of a bar, smelling of one hundred and fifty years of scotch. The walls in here are dark oak and glen plaid. Because, preppy.

There's a tradition at Bryn Mawr of handing down your old or lost or fake driver's license, and I have a confession to make. I am benefiting from that tradition. The bartender tonight is new and there's something sort of lumbering about him. He's not unattractive. You get the feeling he might own a cat. Sensitive.

At first, it's just the two of us making small talk. But then an unusual kind of guy for a place like this comes swaggering in. He's squat and wearing a suit, tie loosened and face red. He definitely looks like he's had enough to drink already.

"Whiskey. Neat."

The bartender nods, pours him a drink. There's a heaviness to the room now. The bartender steps out, to do whatever bartenders do, maybe call his cat sitter.

The ruddy-faced guy turns to me.

"Whassa pretty gal like you doing all alone?"

This is the kind of person I spend my life avoiding. Red-faced and gin-blossomed. Entitled.

I shrug. This means, *Stop talking*.

"You got a boyfriend?"

Ugh. I barely shake my head no. Please stop talking. Please come back, bartender.

"Ya want one?"

He smiles sloppy, leaning in.

Oh God.

"Look, um, I'm really not interested . . ."

He should've known that from all the signals I was giving, but nooooo, he had to make me say it.

And now he's mad.

"Fine. Like I was interested anyway. You're not even that hot, sugar-tits."

Well, this is relaxing. The idea here was that I was going to go to a quiet place and be alone/not alone, but now I get to be hit on and then insulted by a drunk lobster. Ain't being a girl just grand?

I'm not just annoyed now; I'm mad. I'm actually mad for every girl in every public space that has to put up with this hit-on/insult combo. It's unbearable because you can't win, you don't want it, you don't ask for it, but it happens every time. Not just in a bar. Walking down the street. And it happens to all of us.

I turn to the man.

"My tits aren't made of sugar."

I down my drink.

"You're thinking of my *chocha*."

I gesture pantsward. And then I walk by this douchebag and out the door, and there is nothing more satisfying in the whole world.

Yes, I know that was kind of extreme, but *fuck that guy.*

I'm halfway out the posh but understated lobby of the Tillington Hotel when I see him.

The suit.

Not the drunk suit. The skinny suit. From the interview. Sitting down.

What was his name?

Madden.

Fine. I am revved up, and it's obvious that fate has put him in my path for a reason.

It's time for some clarity.

8

Hey! Nice fake interview, *psycho*."

He smiles at that. I should just walk past him and call the police, but somehow my feet have another idea.

"I knew that might seem strange."

"Strange? Oh, no. No, it's totally fine. I go to fake military-industrial-complex interviews every day."

"Touché."

His laptop sits on the table. He turns it toward me and there's video there, on pause. He presses play.

"This is my favorite part." He smiles, looking at the screen.

It takes me a second to realize that's a surveillance video of a girl, in a fight, in a restaurant waiting area.

And that girl is me.

"What the—"

"This part's not bad either."

He points at the screen as I flip Hot Dog over my shoulder.

I can't help but watch as the video plays out. All the way to the end, to the part when I walk out the front door of the Applebee's.

"Nice line, by the way."

"Excuse me?"

"About George Washington. Nice touch."

I look at him. Am I dreaming this? I mean, seriously, WTF? I'm starting to feel seriously unsafe.

"Okay, I'm calling the police now."

"Good luck."

There's something about this guy, a kind of calm, easy confidence that doesn't point to itself but nevertheless somehow prevails.

Maybe it's a trick, but for some reason I'm not scared of him. By all accounts, I should be. Considering he's stalking me in a quite specific way.

"Right. So, I'm leaving. Nice to see you again, weird stalking person. I have no doubt the next sound you hear will be the opening line of your Miranda rights."

Again, he smiles.

"Don't you want to know how I got this?"

Well, he's got me there. Because I definitely *do* want to know that. Along with a bunch of other things.

"Maybe."

"Well, for your information, this was up on YouTube. One hundred hits before it was brought to my attention and I took it down. You're welcome."

"Brought to your attention?"

"Unless, of course, you were hoping to become a viral sensation, which I think might have been quite possible. Sorry if I thwarted your dreams."

"Okay, number one: What are you talking about? And number two . . . *What are you talking about?*"

"I'm talking about a girl who speaks five languages, is a black belt in jujitsu, has a rather high IQ—"

"It's Eskrima. And, wait, how do you know my IQ? I certainly didn't put *that* in my résumé."

He grins like some kind of Brooks Brothers–styled Cheshire cat.

"This is a giant bluff. You're making it all up."

"One fifty-three."

"What?"

"Your IQ score was one fifty-three. You took the test when you were four. In Berkeley. In two thousand one. Before September eleventh, of course."

"Okay, so this is getting weird, and I am officially going."

I walk out the front doors of the Tillington and make a quick break to the right. I should've known this guy was a sociopath. He probably has a basement full of human organs in mason jars. Somewhere in the background, lots of hooks and pulleys. What was I thinking, engaging him like that?

I'm halfway to campus when I look back. No one there. Either I lost him or he didn't bother. Not sure why.

I'm still paranoid walking all the way across the green, the moon shining through the leaves, a canopy above. Not until I lock the dorm door behind me do I let myself breathe a sigh of relief.

It's a long hall and then a left to my room. And that would be peaceful and quiet except I turn the corner and he jumps out at me.

"Boo!"

I jump five miles into the air.

It's not the sociopath, thank God.

It's bachelor number one. Aaron.

"Good evening, fine lass. I am here to solve the mystery of the missing freshman, aka you."

"Jesus, you scared me. Don't do that. I think I might have just died for two seconds."

"These are the consequences of unanswered texts. And now, to your room!"

It's hard not to like Aaron. He definitely rolled an

eighteen in charisma. Yes, that's a Dungeons & Dragons reference. Don't judge me.

Before I know it, Aaron is making out with me up against the wall. And that's okay. In fact, that was what I wanted.

A boy. A distraction.

And still, I can't stop thinking about that stupid sociopath.

9

This is what it looks like. My dream. I'm out in the middle of a wide, black ocean. In a tiny little boat, the sky is twinkling a million stars and everything is kind of glimmering.

I look out over miles and miles of gentle sea, almost like a pane of black glass, spread out. Not a cloud in the sky. But the air is cold. There's a chill, and I can see my breath. My lips are purple. I am in myself and out of myself. First, I am me, then I am looking at me, and back again.

I squint out over the horizon and see land. Land! I catch my breath. I grab the oars and try to steer toward the land. But there's no reason to. The wind is behind me, drifting me there slowly, gently.

As I get closer to the land I realize it's not land at all, but an archipelago of little islands, hundreds of them, the sea drifting among them.

Then. I get even closer and realize that is not a collection of little islands. That is a collection of bodies. Thousands of them. A kind of floating graveyard.

And now my tiny wooden boat is going through them, making a river of space through them, and I try not to look.

They are horrible. Purple faces, open eyes, staring up at me. Their mouths agape.

And I want to scream or cry out or do something, but there's nothing I can do. No sound is coming out. I'm silenced.

And then a body drifts into the side of the boat and I see who it is.

My father.

Drifting in the sea of bodies past me, and I go to try to catch him or do something but he drifts on, drifts past, away into the tide of lost souls. And then she drifts by, too.

My mother.

Her eyes staring up at me. Her long beige hair like sea-weed flowing out from around her head.

And that is the moment I wake up with a gasp. I wake up, my whole body covered in sweat, shivering and choking down the air.

For a minute I feel like this bed is a raft, like I'm still in the dream.

But the walls come back in and the floor and my phone on the bedside table.

Three a.m.

The witching hour.

Three a.m. is the best time to hold whoever is in your bed like you're holding on to a life raft.

Three a.m. is why you call that person in the first place.

10

Four days later I get a note from the dean. I'm supposed to meet him in Royce Hall on Tuesday. That's the administration building. I had my admissions interview there, but that's usually the only time any student sets foot in there.

I can't help but wonder what it's all about. Is there something wrong? Did I *do* something wrong? My imagination teams up with my neurosis to think of all the myriad ways I could be in trouble. So far the only thing I can think of is that fake ID. It can't have to do with my grades or my curriculum. No one is as anal as me when it comes to making sure everything is by the book, all *T*s crossed, all *I*s dotted.

But there it is, the nonspecific note to meet the dean.

"Maybe they want to award you the Weirdest Girl at Bryn Mawr prize."

That's Teddy. Who happens to be lying in his bed in his underwear. I know because I'm lying beside him. In my underwear.

"Thank you. That is very flattering."

"Maybe they want to offer you some kind of grant or something. I mean, aren't you, like, little miss four-point-oh or whatever?"

He leans in to kiss my neck. "Maybe like a sexy grant. Because you're so sexy. Like a grant to have sex with me."

"Hmm. That sounds like a prestigious award."

"Oh, it is. Highly prized. The only thing higher is the Girlfriend Grant. You should try to go for that. The only requisite is meeting the parents."

I look at him. He raises an eyebrow.

Teddy wants me to be his girlfriend. He wants this because he is a Nice Boy from California with a mother who raised him well. He's healthy and able to make normal connections with other human beings.

Fascinating, isn't it?

"I would be honored to be offered that grant, but I'm unsure if I'd be able to meet the requirements."

He rolls his eyes and gets up to close the window.

"Getting kind of cold in here."

I think that meant a lot of things at once. When he comes back he's WAY on the other side of the bed. No more human contact.

Okay, then. The solace of the screen! Back to binge-watching *Borgen*. It's a Danish series we both somehow got addicted to. I don't know how because the description sounds incredibly boring and the show moves at a rate that a snail could outpace. But boy, are we hooked.

It's three hours later when I emerge from his dorm, well versed in the ins and outs of Danish parliamentary politics.

I'm halfway across the green when Patrice appears. A scarf casually yet perfectly draped around his shoulders and neck, of course. I think he was born in that scarf. He looks very serious. Somber.

"Patrice?"

He raises his hand in listless greeting.

"Why are you here? Are you okay?"

"Yes. Um, is it okay? I have something to tell you."

"Um. Sure. What is it?"

"I am breaking up with you."

"Wait! What? Why didn't you tell me?!"

He looks confused.

"I am telling you now."

"But . . . why?"

"Because you are too American."

"Are you serious? I speak five languages! I detest chain restaurants. I—"

"You are more American than you think."

"Oh, really? How so?"

"Everything is disposable to you. There is no heart. Nothing. Just accomplishments. *En fait*, you are neurotic about those accomplishments. It's all you think about. You cannot live in the moment. You won't let yourself. You are too busy thinking about the future. Trying to control it. But, you see, there is no control. There is nothing. There is no past. There is no future. There is only now."

Wow. I guess he's been thinking about this for a while. This little speech is . . . really something.

"Okay . . . anything else?"

"I have met someone. She is French."

"Oh."

"I am sorry."

"Does *she* speak five languages?"

"No."

"How many languages does she speak?"

"French. And a little bit of English."

"Ha!"

"You see? That is the most infantile response I can imagine. You really are a true American."

"You know what? Fine. Yankee Doodle. Grand Old Flag.

Coca Cola, whatevs. Give me Starbucks or give me death! You're right. I'm crazy for all of it. Whereas you are just crazy. Thanks for the heads-up or whatever."

He nods and walks off.

"You should really teach her to speak English!" I yell across the green. "It's the language of commerce! And science! And petrodollars! You realize how important petrodollars are, don't you? They're why we toppled Saddam and Gaddafi! And that's just for starters!"

He rolls his eyes and walks off.

Well, fine. Fine! If he wants to go be French with some French girl, that's fine with me. They can eat baguettes and cook snails and despise Americans together.

I shouldn't care. There's no reason to care. He wasn't even my boyfriend.

"It's just your ego, Paige," I tell myself. "That's all. This is ego."

Someone walks by while I'm talking to myself.

I wave halfheartedly. "Hi there. Just talking to myself."

They don't acknowledge me.

Something is starting to happen where my chest isn't working to bring in air, and now I'm trying harder to bring that air in and that's just making it worse. I used to have this growing up. I'd just start hyperventilating when something was bothering me. Half the time I wouldn't know what it was. My mom would have to talk me off the cliff.

"Breathe, Paige. Just take a deep breath. There. There. In through your nose, out through your mouth. Good. Now again."

She'd stay with me.

"Okay, let's try counting to ten with this. I'll count. Ten deep breaths. Here we go . . ."

When I was five my parents got this picture book that showed you how to "Name it. Tame it. Reframe it." They read it to me a couple of times and then afterward the three of us discussed it. We talked about times something had bothered us and what was *really* the matter and helpful ways to think about it.

This is how conscientious they were and how they taught me: with patience.

With kindness.

And I miss them.

11

Tonight is the spring step sing, which is basically the spring version of Lantern Night. I know. I'll get to it . . .

So, Bryn Mawr has, essentially, a lot of traditions. When folks get accepted, part of the jumping for joy is the *traditions*.

The biggest, most impressive of these, is Lantern Night. Where all the freshmen get a wrought-iron lantern the specific color for their class. You are not allowed to lose your lantern. No one ever loses their lantern. Losing your lantern would be like losing your engagement ring. Or your diploma. Or your dog.

Now, my class color is red, which is all right with me because it means I can sing "Put on the red light" while holding up my lantern. That is from a song called "Roxanne," by the Police. My mom was a fan. Which means she played them all the time, before losing the record, CD, MP3 player, or whatever else it is possible to lose. As discussed: my mom, really good at losing things.

So . . . the fall Lantern Night is the big shebang. Everybody has to go to the cloisters and, under cover of night, sing all sorts of Latin songs that it is a requirement to learn. "Dona Nobis Pacem" is always on the list. But the spring step sing is when we all take our lanterns and, once again, sit on the gray stone steps in the Gothic quad and sing our respective school songs.

I know what you're thinking.

You can't believe I'm doing this. This goofy Hogwarts shit.

Look, I don't blame you. I know it sounds silly.

The thing is . . . it's actually really beautiful with the hundreds of lanterns flickering and the moon coming out over Clock Tower. And the chorus of Latin and Greek songs, sometimes in a round.

Right now, they are singing "Pallas Athena." Actually, *we* are.

It sort of starts as a romp and then goes into these dulcet tones, almost like a lullaby.

Pallas Athena thea,
Mate mato kai sthenou,
Se par he meie I man
Hie ru sou sai soi deine.
Pallas Athena thea,
Mathe mastos kai stenous,
Se par he meie I man

Now comes the slow part:

Hie ru sou sai soi deine.

This part here, this last part, is the heartbreaker:

Akoue, Akoue.

That last part, practically a lullaby.

Pallas Athena, goddess of learning and strength,
We come to worship you, dread goddess.
Bless us we pray; give us wisdom.
Be with us always. Blessed goddess, hear!
Sanctify our lanterns now, to shine forever clearly,
Lighting the way, making bright the dark.

As I'm looking around me at the sea of red, green, light and dark blue lanterns and the black silhouette of the trees against the cobalt blue sky . . . the song somehow travels up through my body in a process of emotional osmosis and, out of nowhere, my face is covered in tears. A river of tears as the song turns into the most gentle lullaby. No one next to me seems to notice. But maybe it's happening to them, too. Maybe we are each in the middle of our own personal revelation, our moment of surrender to all of the things we squelch down during the day. All the things we cover with paperwork and to-do lists and Post-its.

Athena won't let us do that this evening. Somehow she beckons and insists.

I want to cover my face, or disappear, but the only thing I can do is keep singing and letting the sounds of "Pallas Athena" reach down under all the defenses and fly my soul up through the branches and beyond the trees, all the way past the constellations, not even looking back at the moon.

12

Royce Hall, aka the dean's lair, doesn't look like the rest of the campus. It's not gray Gothic architecture with spires and gargoyles like everything else around here. It's a Colonial white house with black shutters and a red door for pizzazz. Apparently, there used to be a farm here, and this was the main house. I don't see a barn anywhere, so I guess they leveled that. Too bad—a barn could have made a pretty cool art studio. Maybe with vaulted ceilings and skylights every-where. The kind of place you could put a pottery wheel.

The bright-red door to Royce Hall is ajar, and I poke my head in. Lots of books and folders everywhere and layers of dust. Dust through the air in a triangle, coming in through

the sunlit window. No people. No one. Not even a recep-
tionist.

I walk up the narrow staircase, the steps creaking under
me, to the second-story landing. Across the hall is the door
for the dean's office, also ajar.

The dean turns to look at me and motions me in. She's
wearing a pencil skirt, her hair in a bun, sensible heels.

As I walk in, she sits down behind her mahogany desk
and offers me a seat in a forest-green patterned wingback
chair.

It's not until I sit down that I realize the other chair is
occupied.

By the sociopath from LexCorp.

13

"You have GOT to be kidding me."

Normally, I would swear, but, let's be honest, this is the dean.

Madden stays quiet, respectful, lets the dean take the lead.

"Ms. Nolan. Paige. I wanted you to make the acquaintance of a colleague of mine. Madden Carter."

I look over at the sociopath. He's not as smug as he should be, considering.

"Um, yes, we've met. Briefly."

"Right. Well, Madden and I go way back, to Exeter actually, and he assures me he has important business with you."

"Business?"

"Yes. Business."

This is too weird. I can't even look at this guy. All of a sudden I feel like I'm in that movie with the devil baby where everyone in the building turns out to be in cahoots.

"Anyway, I'll leave you two to discuss things in private."

She nods to Madden, then to me, before walking out and leaving me totally alone with him, here in our respective green snooty chairs. Not cool. I mean, probably not even legal. I am seventeen! *In loco parentis* and all of that?

"Okay, I know this is a bit extreme, but I cannot keep chasing you all around Timbuktu and having you run away each time. I am not a psycho. I am not stalking you. I assure you."

"I am tentatively but hesitantly listening. Out of respect for the dean."

"Okay. Allow me to explain. We are very interested in you. In your talent."

"Talent?"

"*Talent's* not exactly the right word. Ability."

"Wait. Who, exactly, is this 'we'? You and your pimp friends?"

"Pimp . . . ? No. We, in this case, are a government intelligence-gathering agency."

"Ha! Right. Like what, the CIA?"

"No, we are not the CIA. And I am not joking."

"Ah, so you're FBI."

"Actually, no."

"Okay, well, I don't really believe you, so you might as well tell me who you are—or, in this case, who you are pretending to be."

"RAITH."

"Excuse me?"

"An operational intelligence organization. Reconnaissance and Intelligence AuTHority. R.A.I.T.H."

"That acronym totally makes no sense."

He shrugs. "I wasn't in charge of branding."

"RAITH. So I suppose its mission is to travel through the fires of Mordor and retrieve a magical yet corrupting ring?"

"Come again?"

"RAITH. That is a *Lord of the Rings* reference."

"Never saw it."

"Now I *know* you're a psycho. And the correct answer is *never read it. As in, I have never read the entire J. R. R. Tolkien* Lord of the Rings *series and then avidly gone to see the films with initial excitement and then, through the years, a bit of disappointment.*"

"Okay, I have neither read the *Lord of the Rings* books nor seen the films."

"One more question."

"Yes."

"Are you a robot?"

"Very amusing."

"I just can't believe you've never seen or read *The Lord of the Rings* unless you're a cyborg. Which is okay, by the way. I, too, plan on either downloading my consciousness onto a non-carbon-based life-form or injecting nanobots into my brain so that I'll be able to manifest superintelligence and ultimate cyberconnectivity. That is, if the singularity is actually a positive thing, in the more optimistic Ray Kurzweil version of the world. However, there is always the possibility that the rise of artificial intelligence will go a little more the way Stephen Hawking predicted, where humanity will be in such a rush to master artificial intelligence that no one will stop to actually program the AI not to harm us, i.e., that won't be a fundamental, seminal part of their code, so that when AI inevitably reaches superintelligence, we will all be wiped out as the superintelligent AI realizes we are a hindrance to whatever random programming goal the AI might have been given. Like being the most efficient letter-writing robot, or something equally banal."

Madden is just looking at me now.

"And you're asking me if *I'm* the robot?"

"Well, it is worth contemplating. Since it involves the possibility of an extinction event."

"This rebel-without-a-cause act . . ."

"How do you know it's an act?"

"That's essentially what I'm asking."

"Am I a true rebel, is that your question? Welp, I was just broken up with by a Parisian for being *too* American. Whatever that means."

"So . . . let me get this straight . . . having your own opinion and always questioning the world around you, having the freedom to criticize your country and continually striving to make the world a better place . . . you don't think that's part of being an Ameri—"

"Depends on who you're criticizing. What about JSOC? What about KBR?"

"It's people like you who ask these questions that make this country what it is."

"Now you're just flattering me. You want something. Clearly."

"Yes, we do. We want you, Paige. We want you to join."

"Your specter league of fake intelligence?"

"Yes. Except it's not fake."

"So I'd be working for the government?"

"Yes."

I turn to him. "How do I know you're not just some lunatic with delusional disorder? You know this is the kind of thing people walk across the street talking to themselves

about, right? Top secret government agencies that *ooooo*
nobody knows about 'cause of their *ooooo* double triple secret
mission and *ramble ramble ramble*."

"Understandable, your doubt."

He takes out his phone and scrolls to a picture of him
standing there next to the president. It's an incredibly stellar
fake.

"Yeah, I use Photoshop, too. If you like, I can show you a
picture of Jesus and me surfing."

Madden rolls his eyes, looks back at his phone, and dials.

"Would you like to speak to her? The president, I mean.
She went to a Seven Sisters college, too, you know."

I can hear the phone dialing and then a click, and an
unmistakable voice on the other end says, "Madden?" Before
I know it, I lunge, disconnecting the call.

"You just hung up on the leader of the free world."

He dials the number back, off speaker, and appears to
make some chitchat. Some apologies.

I barely hear any of it because suddenly the floor around
us is spinning and the molding on the walls is a crisscross of
bars on a kind of ivy-covered carnival ride.

He hangs up. "Told her it was a butt dial. She was very
understanding."

I blink. "Let me get this straight. You are telling me that
the government wants to recruit me for some black ops–type,

probably illegal mission *and* that you just said the word *butt* to the actual president of the United States?"

"I am."

"You want me to work for *the government*. The same government that I tried to contact over and over about my parents for the past two years and have not heard back from once, not one time, except for the initial cursory so-sorry-your-parents-are-lost, the-politics-in-the-region-are-complicated, so-sorry-we-don't-negotiate-with-terrorists, oh-well phone call . . ."

I don't tell him the part about lying in bed awake at night for six weeks straight, bawling, sweating, screaming into my pillow, waiting to hear back from someone, anyone, always a different person, always a different department, about whether my parents were alive or dead, where they may or may not have been, whether they could get them back or whether they would try to get them back. I don't tell him about the maddening uncertainty, realizing I am alone in the world and desperately clinging to my sheets, feeling like I am capsizing, a teetering, puzzled pawn in a maze on a sinking bureaucratic ship.

". . . That same government?!"

"Yes."

"Well, dearest fake spy boss, I would rather peel my skin off and feed it to the Tea Party."

And with that I stand up. I will march out over those

creaky floors, down that too-thin staircase, out the bright-red door, and into the sunset.

Whatever that sociopath was talking about, I want nothing to do with it. Nothing to do with him, nothing to do with secret made-up shadow organizations, nothing to do with shilling for the government.

That government abandoned my parents.

That government left them for dead.

Of course, when I get to the door, it's locked.

"Okay, seriously, what the fuck?"

14

"Why is this door locked, and where is the black-ops heli-copter to spirit me away to Guantanamo Bay, where I will receive no due process but might possibly write a bestselling tell-all novel?"

"Sorry, that was a fluke. Here."

Madden lets me out and shrugs, innocent.

"Okay, for the record, I do not believe for an instant that was some wacky mishap. But fine. See you in the Matrix or whatever."

He waves me out. "No hijinks. You're free to go."

Except . . .

I don't even make it to the green by the time he catches

up with me. Rhoads dorm has a gray stone arch in the middle of it, almost like a gate to the rest of the campus. And it's under this arch that everything changes.

"Paige, stop. Just listen to me."

"Jesus. Seriously? You're, like, obsessed. Just leave me alone."

He stops.

"Paige, there's something you should know. But I can't tell you if you keep running away."

I'm looking at him now and sizing him up. He's calm. Relieved. Kind of like a guy who has just shown his cards.

The campus center café is a dorky place, but there's something about it I find soothing. It's steps away from my dorm, so it's my main source of caffeine. And study breaks. And procrastination. It's an airy place with high ceilings and pale birch booths. It is supposed to be calming.

Madden is sitting across from me in the booth. Luckily, there's practically no one in here, so the great possibility of me bawling my face off is slightly remedied.

Now in front of me, on the table, they start to come. First, their passport photos. My mother. My father. Both of them looking just a little younger than when I last saw them. My dad, in an olive-green button-down with epaulets. My mom, with a scarf. Now this. This next picture. Grainier. A black-and-white picture taken from far away.

And the wind is knocked out of me.

It's some kind of camp. Some kind of enclosure. There's a yard, pale, filled with dust, a large fence around it. Near the corner of the yard, as if just arrived, stand two figures, one taller, one slight. In front of them two men are turned to each other, having what looks like an argument. Even though their faces are blindfolded and their hands are tied, I know it. I know this is them. My mother and father. Standing there. In this horrible place.

There it is. My chest. Unable to breathe. The air just sitting there in the room, but not for me. Impossible.

Madden looks at me, concerned.

"Breathe, okay? Just listen to me."

I try to slow down, take my eyes off the photograph.

"Five of us were assigned," he says. "Most of us were young, new. It didn't bother me, our inexperience. We had good intelligence. We knew where they were. We were sent to extricate them."

These words, these words are falling down and some of them are landing, some of them are landing in my head, some are going straight to my heart, others to the bottom of my belly. What to do with these words? What am I supposed to do with these words?

"We trained in a mocked-up model of the site. Kind of like a movie set, built based on satellite images. We planned for everything."

And now I'm looking down at five files. Each one has a photograph in the corner. Each one in their dress blues, an official photograph, light-blue background, flag in the back— red, white, and blue.

"Except our Seahawk taking fire from antiaircraft launchers seized from the Iraqis. Our helicopter crashed."

And now I'm looking at a picture of four caskets, draped in the flag, a cargo plane in the background.

And now it hits me.

"We? You were . . ."

"I'm the only one who made it out."

There was life in this room a second ago. There was something moving. But now it's just still. Just silence in a seemingly empty room.

I shuffle back to the photographs, the dress blues, the SEALs. There, younger and much more luminous somehow, is Madden, with crew-cut hair, seeming almost like a boy. Happy.

I look again at the photograph of my parents. There in a dusty corner halfway across the world.

"They're alive, Paige." The ground falls out from under me.

I can't breathe suddenly. That dream I had. The one with the ocean of bodies. I thought it meant they were gone. That somehow I *knew*. But now the truth comes in like a comet.

And now it bursts into flame.

I pick up the photograph of my parents, touch my fingers to their out-of-focus outline, wishing I could just grab them, grab them right out of there through the photograph.

"Are you sure?" It's a whisper. "How? Why?"

"We don't know. Your father's work on the Middle East is highly respected in the Arab world. There could be something there."

"But they kill journalists all the time. In horrible ways."

I'm still recovering. They're alive. My parents are alive.

All of a sudden the colors have come back into the room. I realize there are paintings on the walls I've never seen before. And an intricate, hundred-light sculpture, made of glass, hanging in the cavernous space. I never noticed that either.

Beauty. Beauty in the world.

"This mission. To save your parents. I asked to lead it. I read their books. In Annapolis. The world needs to question the dominant paradigm."

The dominant paradigm. It's a quote from *River to Sea*, my dad's bestseller.

When my mom and dad went missing, it was all over the news.

Their pictures were plastered all over the papers and the TV and the internet for a few days.

And then there was another one of those mass shootings. This one at a Walmart in Arkansas. And that became what was plastered all over the papers and the TV and the internet. Then a pop star released a surprise album.

And poof, my parents were gone. No more story. Like they vanished from the earth.

"The safe return of your parents is a matter of utmost importance," Madden whispers. "This mission came down all the way from the White House."

"I don't believe you."

"Well, then you don't know our president very well." He smirks, waggles his phone. "You can trust me. I have her on speed dial."

Okay.

We sit there for a moment, me wanting to ask this question yet being afraid, *terrified*, of the answer.

"Everyone at the checkpoint died. In the midst of the confusion, the fog of war, your parents escaped."

"How?"

"We don't really know how. Quite frankly, it seems impossible."

"So you don't know where they are now?"

"We're gathering intel."

"So they're just out somewhere, in the middle of all this ISIS terror, in the middle of all these drone strikes and the Russians fucking bombing everything in sight, by themselves?!"

"I know. I know you're worried."

The color comes out of the room again. Everything returns to beige and gray. I feel . . . heavy.

"Paige, you can help. We need you."

"You're joking, right? What am *I* supposed to do?"

"We're going to find them. Wherever they are. And when we do, we'll bring them home. You and me."

"Me?"

"Yes, you. With me. I'm keeping this mission alive. Not just for your parents. For *them*." He gestures to the pictures. "For their families."

Those four faces are staring up at me. The Navy SEALs. They had parents, too. Three of them had children. Small children. There's a photograph of one of them, a little towhead with bright-blue eyes, staring up from a birthday cake, smiling, with blue frosting all over her mouth. The candle on the cake says 3. Behind her, her daddy holds her on his lap, beaming. Smiling bright.

In the little girl's eyes there is only light.

There's a picture of me at my third birthday somewhere.

I looked like her once.

"When do I start?"

INTERLUDE
I

This is what it looks like. The report. Tucked into the seventh page of the Moscow Times. A mere paragraph.

It says only that shots were fired and several injured two hours outside of Moscow at the dacha of a noted Muscovite, Thursday night, at approximately nine p.m. It says there was a subsequent exchange of gunfire. It does not say the how, it does not say the why, and, most important, it does not say the who.

No, it does not say who happened to be at that particular dacha when chaos, gunfire, and general mayhem erupted.

Because if it had said the who, well, then it would have not been neatly tucked on the seventh page of the Moscow Times. No, no. If it had said the who, it would have been front page of the New York Times. Cover story. Photo before the fold.

But come with me. I'll show you.

1

You know how in movies they'll insert a training session, with a power ballad blasting over a testosterone-happy montage? And they'll show the down-and-out, kind of pudgy protagonist beat up a cow carcass in some meat-packed freezer in an undisclosed location? And then at the end of three minutes he just sort of emerges as Hercules? Welp, that's because to actually show anyone training for an extended period of time, or any period of time for that matter, is about as exciting as watching grass grow. Even if it's for a covert government intelligence agency. Scratch that. *Especially* if it's for a covert government intelligence agency.

"Again," Madden snaps.

I'm not in a fish tank, ladies and gentlemen, but I am in

an enormous lap pool, the sounds echoing off the cavernous tile. There's no marker on the entrance to this entire complex, or on many of the buildings, but if there was I would call this one "Super Secret Spy Swimming Complex" or SSSSC, for short. We've been in here all morning, me swimming freestyle, trying to better my time, Madden standing there, by the edge of the pool, making me feel like a guppy.

"Is this the kind of thing where you work me so hard that I fall apart and then you put me back together again in the form of a Madden-bot who will just shoot first and ask questions later?"

"It's possible." Madden smirks.

And I start my next lap. Each lap, trying to beat my own time, competing against myself.

This is my summer. Or "How I Spent My Summer Vacation."

Not parties and hangovers and a Pasolini *Trilogy of Life* marathon featuring Il Decameron with bachelor number two. (Oh, you don't know Pasolini's Decameron? That's because you forgot to be a pretentious person with a love of completely toneless films that fluctuate blindingly among sex, slapstick, and scatological humor.) Nope. No obscure film marathons *this* summer! This, instead, is the summer when sort-of-cute-but-way-too-square Madden insists I can hold my breath for thirty minutes, run a mile in three minutes, and tell pithy jokes, in fluent Russian, immediately after I do both. Right now he is insisting I can swim the one-hundred-meter freestyle in less than ninety seconds. To give you some perspective, Michael Phelps got it in forty-seven.

I know you think there's a Bond villain above me maniacally stroking a white cat before pushing a button to send in five great white sharks to devour me. And at this point I wouldn't mind that, really. Not now that I have practically morphed into a fish and grown fins, and the ache of my upper back and arms will probably last until 2020. So, given all of that, you can see why I welcome death. But it is not an evil villain torturing me. Nope. It's Madden. He's still insisting on the hundred meter in less than ninety seconds. He's lost his marbles, clearly.

"One hundred and thirteen seconds."

"I am in extreme dislike . . ."

Gasp.

". . . of this process at the present moment."

Gasp.

"And, also, of you . . ."

Gasp.

". . . in a dispassionate sort of way."

Madden raises an eyebrow.

"Methinks the lady doth protest too much."

"Methinks you just like annoying me in my bathing suit.

Admit it, *you* couldn't do this."

"Wanna bet?"

"Please."

And, wouldn't you know it, before I know what's happening, Madden has decided to strip down to his skivvies and proceed to jump into the pool.

I, on the other hand, am busy pretending not to notice that he is—okay, seriously, completely—in perfect, not-too-muscular/not-too-scrawny shape. With stripes on his tummy. I think it's called a six-pack. But I'm not noticing any of that. Nope. Instead, I am pretending to admire the blue-and-white plastic buoys separating each lane.

"These blue-and-white plastic thingies are really interesting. I wonder who invented them?"

SPLASH.

That's Madden. In the pool swimming headfirst to the other side and back before I can finish this sentence.

There. See. He's already back.

I'm still pretending not to notice his body, which a lesser female might, say, throw herself on top of.

"It doesn't seem like anyone would actually need these blue-and-white plastic buoys not to run into each other, but perhaps on the off chance they became delirious or specially unaware—"

"Paige. What are you talking about?"

"Oh, I'm actually just wondering about the levels of chlorine in the pool right now. When was the last time you guys had them checked? Have you considered a saltwater pool? It's really much better for the—"

He smiles. Gets out of the pool. Proud of himself.

I just lost my train of thought.

"You can get out. You're done for the day."

"Already? It's only midnight."

"See you at oh-five-hundred."

"Just say five a.m. It's not like we're in Beirut."

There's a moment in the middle of my own personal pool exit and towel-drying when my spidey senses tingle. It seems like I might actually, honestly, catch him ogling me.

I turn.

But no. He's looking away.

Anyway, I'm not disappointed. Because it's not like I care. I mean, why would I care? Just stop it.

After a quick shower in the bleach-flavored locker room consisting of a criminal amount of chemicals, I exit my government-sponsored pseudo-YMCA only 80 percent poisoned.

There goes my phone. A text from Aaron. It reads simply: ?

Well done, Aaron. One lone question mark. Did you know English was actually a language once?

His competitor for my cold and lifeless heart, Teddy, has gone back to Santa Monica for the summer, where his effortlessly attractive self is free to bask in perfect weather, unencumbered by a phenomenally imperfect, emotionally disassociated, soon-to-be covert government operative, whom he has, judging by a recent Facebook unfriending and Twitter unfollowing, unceremoniously broken up with. It's okay. I get it. I'd give up on me, too. (Although Teddy really was the best one of the lot. One day, he'll make some perfect girl very happy. She'll be named something like Abigail. I'll see their wedding pictures in my Facebook feed and cry into my vegan chocolate chip cookie ice cream.)

This leaves only Aaron. The last holdout.

You remember those scenes in all those aforementioned training montages where you see the sweaty protagonist watching French surrealist cinema with his love interest? No? Do you know why? Because Rocky Balboa does not watch *The Discreet Charm of the Bourgeoisie*. I know. You're surprised.

Rocky Balboa has done so much training that the montage did not show you that Luis Buñuel is like a fast-acting narcotic on his brain and makes him fall heavily asleep, *avec* snoring. And likely drool.

Look. This whole now-I'm-an-international-spy thing isn't

really going to jibe with Aaron. Now that I think of it, I kind of have to dump him.

I just don't know how to do it.

Hi, Aaron. No, I'm sorry, I can't come over. The thing is, I've kinda been recruited by a covert government organization— No, not the CIA. It's called RAITH. I said RAITH— Yes, like Lord of the Rings *. . . Yeah, I know. I don't know if they got the reference. They're sort of humorless, honestly. You know what? It doesn't matter. The point is, if there's any hope of liberating my parents and possibly saving the world in whatever covert way I might be saving it, I'm not going to be able to take our relationship to the next level.*

Now THAT would be a text.

By the time I get out of the locker room, Madden is long gone. It's okay. It's not like I was expecting him to wait for me and exchange witty banter or ask me out for an impromptu drink or anything.

Jesus. Stop.

I'm totally, *totally* not interested.

2

3:02 a.m.

Fifty Shades of Grey is the name of a book, but it also should be the name of my bedroom at the training facility. Whoever put this together pinned DRAB and METAL on their Pinterest board. Walls: light gray. Door: dark gray. Bed: darker gray. You get the idea. The silver lining here, or rather the gray lining, is that I have my own room. No, we are not all in one room like in *Full Metal Jacket*, with that guy yelling racial epithets at us all day. This is much more chic. Only the best here at RAITH. And by "best" I mean a double shot of depresso.

There's only one other girl here, and she has already

succeeded in putting me to shame on the driving course. I UBER. She's from East Los. Yes, East LA. Viva Martinez. I think she might be the inspiration for *The Fast and the Furious*. Fun fact: she has a purple mohawk. It's a kind of graduated purple that gets darker near the back. Sometimes she wears it spiky. Sometimes she wears it down, in a swoop. Sometimes she even wears it in a braid. Always, she wears it cool. Kudos to you, Need for Speed. You be you.

If you're curious what I'm doing up at three in the morning, the answer is *hyperventilating*. If you're curious why I'm hyperventilating, the answer is I just woke up from the most horrific dream about my mother. And father. Usually, when you wake up from these things, you get to sigh in relief that it was all just a dream. The thing about this is that I really don't know if it is. It could be real. For all we know, it could be exactly this terrifying and unspeakable and inhumane.

In the dream my mother and father were being pulled from each other. My mother was being hurried away into a long line of women and girls and put on a bus. My father was being forced into a long line of men, in front of them a ditch. Behind them were men with guns, dressed in black. My mom watched, screaming, before the horrible thing was about to happen. Before the guns were raised and pointed.

I woke up in a gasp.

It's about two minutes until I realize I am here in this gray room, that it wasn't real.

God, please make it just be a dream.

There is a gray pillow here for me to put my face in, so no one hears me. This isn't even a cry.

This is a prayer.

3

Madden has decided that today would be a good day to humiliate me. Here is what he has cooked up, before breakfast: a predawn romp. It's actually not a romp at all—it's a race. Involving cars. Involving cones. Involving steep turns. Involving competition. And, worst of all, involving me.

I am an excellent driver.

In my mind. When nobody's watching. I could drive circles around you. And even East Los Viva.

However, there is the small issue that in the human realm, when I am driving an actual vehicle, which is rare, and there is someone in the passenger seat, which is even rarer—I have a tendency to get nervous. And a bit neurotic. Okay, fine, let's just face it. I am a terrible driver.

Madden is leading me across a long field to what looks like an obstacle course in a car commercial. A silver sports car sneers out at us from the pavement, two racing stripes over the top.

"Like it? Two thousand sixteen Dodge Viper SRT."

"I don't know what any of that means."

"Six hundred forty-five horsepower, six-hundred-pound-foot torque."

"Are you even speaking English right now?"

We make our way next to the spiffy little thing. Inside, at the wheel, there is Viva, stone-faced.

"C'mon, Paige, admit it. You're impressed."

"If I were to divulge the materialistic side of my consciousness, perhaps."

Madden sizes me up.

"Did you even ever get Christmas presents . . . ?"

"Yes. And Hanukkah presents. And Kwanzaa. Three Kings Day. Also, Saint Lucia Day and Ramadan. It's important not to play favorites. You know . . . you never know who could actually be running this thing . . . probably important not to put all your eggs in one basket—"

"Stop. Stop talking."

Viva steps out of the Viper and gives me a look halfway between charity and sorrow.

"She driving today?"

"Yes, Viva. I'm afraid so. Do you mind riding shotgun?"

"Shotgun? With her?"

"I was hoping you could give her some pointers."

"How about this for a pointer? Don't drive, *juera*."

"Okay, I think that's not entirely fair. Also, you can speak Spanish to me—I'm totally fluent, although my accent is actually Cuban, not Guatemalan, which is what I'm detecting, but neither of us have an actual Spanish accent, from Spain, because let's face it, all that lisping just sounds weird."

"Why are you talking so much?"

Ouch.

She turns to Madden.

"Please don't make me get in the car with her. I have dreams."

Madden smiles. I wouldn't think he would have such a familiar repartee with someone with a purple mohawk.

"I think Viva has a point; there's really no reason for me to drive."

Viva and I both turn to Madden, each of us hoping he will call it a day.

"Nice try, Paige. But you never know. Perhaps you'll learn something."

"And perhaps YOU'LL learn something."

"What is that supposed to mean?"

"I don't know, actually."

Viva throws me some serious shade and heads back to the car.

"Okay, I have a follow-up question."

Madden exhales. "Yes."

"Is this car worth a lot in your human money?"

"Paige, there's nothing around. Okay? You're going to be fine. Just get in the car, turn on the ignition, and do the obstacle course."

"In that order?"

"Yes."

HOOOOOONK.

Inside the car, Viva does the international shrug for *what the F is taking you so long?*

I look across the obstacle course. It's about a mile long and there are a lot of orange cones involved. Out toward the end of the track, there seems to be some kind of wet pavement, but that could easily be a mirage. The sun is just coming up from the east, blanketing the track in a kind of golden matte.

"It's now or never, Paige."

Well, here goes.

4

A 2016 Dodge Viper SRT costs exactly $87,895. I know, because I just crashed one.

Allow me to elaborate.

Before the wet pavement mirage, I was doing pretty well. Yes, there was a lot of nervous chatter coming out of my mouth, but, in general, I was actually kind of getting into the orange cone swerve of it all. To be true, it was exciting. Thrilling!

Viva coaches me. "Okay, push into the curve. That's right. Smooth. You gotta keep it smooth. Never jerky. Jerky is death. Never jerky."

"Jerky is death."

"Yes, confident. Smooth. Push into the turn. No

second-guessing. You can't second-guess. Second-guessing is death."

"Second-guessing is death."

"Exactly. Now do you see that? That's wet concrete. If you lose control on a wet or snowy surface, it can be much harder to regain control. Got it? There is much less traction to work with."

"Much less traction to work with." I repeat her, trying to absorb, nervous.

"Less traction is bad. Losing control with less traction equals death."

"Losing control with less traction equals death. Boy, a lot of things equal death around here."

"That's true, *gringa*. You gotta be doubly careful in the rain or the snow."

"Careful in inclement weather."

"You gotta be smooth. Never jerky. Anything jerky in the rain or the snow equals death."

"Again."

"*Muerto.*"

"Yes. *Muerto*. Got it. *Lo entiendo.*"

"Watch out!"

And this is the part where some sort of decoy, designed to look like a woman crossing the street with her child pops up in front of me and turns what was a pleasant educational

114

session into a careening, out-of-control death trap wherein Viva and I are swerving sideways to miss the sweet family decoy, overcorrecting the other way by about 180 degrees, and fishtailing all the way into the ditch next to the track, which is more like a gravel pit of death.

After what seems like a million hours but is, actually, only about a second, I turn to Viva and see her covered in gravel, dust, and scratches. The crushed tin can around us does not bode well for my insurability. There is nothing moving in Viva's face. Everything is moving under it, simmering.

"Jesus. I am so, so sorry."

"Get out, get out!"

And now Viva is dragging me out of the car and we are looking on. Everything seems pretty normal for a second. Just a crushed can of a car, in a ditch.

And then . . .

"Oh Jesus. RUN!"

Viva hurls me back with her as something in the car catches, and next thing I know, there is a giant explosion behind us and a hot blast of wind propelling us off our feet, into the air, forward, and into the field. Our faces used to have skin on them, but now they are just mostly scrapes and dirt.

Viva also has daggers in her eyes, and they are pointing at me.

Behind her the smoke from the car billows up behind her in red-and-gray plumes.

Madden comes sprinting toward us from the other side of the field. He should be out of breath but he's one of those CrossFit guys, I bet, with some sort of medieval contraption in the basement where he maniacally laughs all night watching *House of Cards*.

"Stay there! They're on their way!"

I'm assuming the *they* in that statement must be the ambulance barreling forward across the track, sirens blaring.

Viva's eyes stay on me. Blades.

"You don't like me very much, do you?"

She exhales, resigned, there in the dust.

"That's okay. I don't like me that much right now either."

5

I'm not sure why anyone on the face of the planet would want to use a bow and arrow. I mean, it seems like a fairly limited field of expertise and usefulness. Unless your name is Katniss.

One hundred feet away from us is a giant bull's-eye. A tiny speck of yellow, circled by red, circled by blue, circled by black. There are five bull's-eyes set up and four other beginning archery students beside me. I got here first, getting dibs on the far end so as to minimize my humiliation. I don't think I need to tell you that it's gotten around about the Viper.

Madden stands beside me, sounding like an instruction manual.

"Always inspect your arrows to make sure they are straight and that each nock is in good working condition. A cracked nock can break when fired from the bow and can cause the bow to 'dry fire.' This can cause injury and will damage the bow."

"Is there a person in there?"

"Yes. Always make sure you know what lies behind your target. Never point your weapon at anything you do not intend to shoot. Arrows travel fast and have a lot of power."

"Thank you. I think I've got it."

"Make sure the arrow is in the nock before shooting; otherwise it can lead to serious injury."

"Got it. The nock."

"Listen to me, Paige. Instinctive shooting is the coordination between the eyes and the bow arm. It allows your experience and subconscious to guide your movement. It requires large amounts of concentration and practice. Focus on nothing but the center of the target."

"Concentration. Yes."

"Are you sure your right is the dominant eye?"

"Yes, of course I'm sure. That was, like, step one, remember?"

"I just want to be sure."

I raise the bow, set in the nock, and shoot.

Black.

Totally not humiliating.

"Not bad. Actually, I thought you might not even hit the target, so this is good."

"Okay, good, are we done?"

"Nice try. Again."

And again, I aim and shoot. This time, blue.

"Better."

"Okay, cool. Ready to go?"

Madden just stares.

"Are you planning on sending me into a kind of dome where I have to kill all my friends with only this weapon to save me?"

"Amusing. Again."

I raise my bow, concentrate, and shoot. Blue again.

"Okay, let's try for yellow this time."

"Um, yellow is a bull's-eye."

"Always aim for the bull's-eye, Paige."

"Well, duh. I'm just saying don't hold your breath."

Again, I raise the arrow in the nock, aim, concentrate, and shoot.

Red! Dang it. So close!

"Keeping doing that for an hour. I'll be back at noon."

"What? An hour? What is this even for? Unless you have a time machine and are sending me back to . . . Wait a minute. DO you have a time machine?"

"Of course. I'm actually from the fortieth century."

"Does the singularity begin in two thousand forty-three or does artificial intelligence eradicate humanity?"

"We eradicate humanity. What do you think of my human skin?"

"Too white."

"Of course. See you in an hour."

I call after him as he walks away, "You know this is sort of a pointless exercise, right? Like underwater basket weaving or Candy Crush or that game where the participants are meant to throw an orange inflatable orb into a wire circle placed parallel to the earth."

"You mean basketball."

"Oh! Is that what it's called?!"

Even though it's too cold out here and I really would prefer to go inside and collapse for ten hours, there's something about being in this space. This space with wet grass and the morning dew. This space with robins chirping. This space—with Madden.

He makes it better.

Even though he's annoying and preppy and square. The air around him, or the way he takes it in, or just to sort of see what he's wearing. He makes it better.

I can never tell him that.

He's halfway across the field now, walking back to

whatever secret operation he's roped someone else into. I don't know why but I catch myself watching him. Glued to him walking across the field, the morning dew a blanket under our feet and the sun casting amber shadow over the stretch of crabgrass.

He turns back.

"Why are you still looking at me?!"

"I'm waiting for you to return to your true robot form!"

6

Viva is sizing me up with pity. The mats below us go red, blue, red, blue, red, the length of the floor, all the way over to the locker room. The sensei here is from Kyoto. Her name is Satchiko. That's Japanese for *girl who brings good luck*.

There's eight other people on the mat, my fellow trainees, watching us, anticipating. I get the feeling they're excited to see Viva make mincemeat out of me. Word not only got around about the Viper . . . it also got around about Viva. So, possibly, there are bets on this thing. Heavy bets.

Satchiko steps back gracefully, with the respect given to the craft.

This is just a standard judo dojo, and I'm pretty sure no one told Satchiko about my Eskrima, jujitsu, aikido, or karate training. That's okay. I don't need to announce myself.

Viva and I face each other. She raises an eyebrow, wondering if I plan on just running off.

I nod.

She approaches me, obligated.

THWAP!

Yes, I just flipped Viva onto the mat. A collective gasp goes through the dojo. Everyone but Satchiko. Satchiko is true Japanese.

Viva looks up at me from the mat.

I can tell she's about to use every curse word in English, Spanish, and Spanglish, but, seeing Satchiko standing there with the gravitas of Mount Fuji, thinks better of it.

She gets up and dusts herself off.

Satchiko gestures for another round.

Viva, again, stands in front of me, this time on edge, ready to pounce.

Satchiko nods and Viva comes crashing toward me.

THWAP!

That one was even harder. That's her fault, actually. I just used her momentum. Again, a collective gasp.

Viva stays on the ground for a second, stunned. Her eyes up at the ceiling. I guess she thought she had that one.

Satchiko nods to me, the signal it's over.

I reach out a hand to help Viva up. She looks at my hand.

I can tell the last thing she wants to do is take it. I get it. I just humiliated her in front of the entire dojo. Sort of like I humiliated myself by crashing that Viper.

Satchiko stands there, calm. "The mountain remains unmoved by its apparent defeat by the mist."

You could imagine the world would blast itself into smithereens and Satchiko would still be standing there like a thousand-year-old willow.

I leave my hand there for Viva.

You may be wondering why I'm not spewing my usual sarcasm all over the place. That's not what you do here. In places like this you aspire to be like Satchiko, quiet as the lake around the golden temple in Kyoto.

Viva takes a deep breath and relents, accepting my hand and my assistance. Once up, she rubs her back and looks at me, curious.

It's okay. I know she thought I was just some dumbass. That's the point, really. Never let them see you coming. There's more to martial arts than just moves. Ask Satchiko.

As we are leaving the dojo, we all nod in respect and walk gently out.

"Arigatōgozaimashita."

It has all been very good with us.

Just as I am stepping out, I hear Satchiko say, *"Jukuren shita taka wa sono kagidzume o kakushi."*

It means:

"A skilled hawk hides its talons."

I relay this to Viva, who is beyond annoyed at everything about me right now.

She rubs her back, mutters, "Yeah. Hides them so well, you mistake them for a turkey."

"Wait. Did you just call me a turkey?"

But I smile. It's the nicest thing I've heard in a while.

7

Strategies for Making Gael García Bernal Fall in Love with Me:

1. Get hit by a car. Lie on the ground in a vaguely ethnic but not too culture-appropriating dress. Perhaps expose one thigh, or at least a knee. Make sure I get hit just so, so that I look disheveled but not like a nightmare horror show with half my face gone. No, no. I have to be in kissable disarray. Just the right amount so he subconsciously thinks of me lying next to him after he's ravaged me. In this arrangement, I imagine the street to be cobblestone. Someone's aunt is hanging laundry in the background.

2. Accidentally become his translator. Insert myself into a situation where he is in a foreign land and in need of

someone to translate between Spanish and Russian (or French or Chinese). It will all seem completely haphazard and meant to be. He will look up at me gratefully, and I will blush. He will find this endearing and invite me to dinner or a drink or maybe just to walk around the park and look lovingly at each other.

3. Stalk him.

I'm fairly sure number three would be the least successful of these plans, but it might be necessary to enact either number one or number two.

Okay, I know you're wondering why I am suddenly obsessed with Gael García Bernal. And I'll be honest with you. It is a bit sudden. See, what happened was . . . I binge-watched. I started with *Mozart in the Jungle*. That was the appetizer. Then I moved on to *Y Tu Mamá También*. That was the entrée. Then *The Motorcycle Diaries*. Clearly, the dessert.

So now I am a lost cause.

In my daydreams, he and I are studying and he is next to me and I am completely nervous and there are butterflies flying all over the place inside my body, and then, this is the best part . . . he and I happen to fall silent for a moment. This is the part when I am wondering if he's in love with me or if I'm just an idiot. And then he kisses me. And it's a long,

127

supersexy kiss, which I am having a hard time focusing on because I am thinking: Please think I'm a good kisser. Please think I'm a good kisser. Please think I'm a good kisser.

That's the end of the daydream.

And I love this daydream. Because this is a reality I would gladly just fly into and never come back from. Like, if God came down and said, *Hello, Paige, my child! Would you like to stay in ACTUAL reality or would you like to stay in THIS Gael García Bernal–kissing reality? Which do you choose . . . for eternity?* I would not take a second before saying, *I'm gonna have to go with Gael, Lord.*

Why do I know this? Well, whenever I have this dream I am hugely disappointed when I wake up. Like *heartbroken.*

Also, now that I've broken up with or gotten broken up with by all my boyfriends, it's really just Gael and me. That's who I daydream about. By myself. During lunch.

Lunch is in a sterile government-issue cafeteria. Right now Madden is walking toward me, plastic tray held before him.

"Daydreaming?"

"Nope. Just strategizing on ways to make Gael García Bernal fall in love with me."

"Excuse me?"

"We haven't reached the making-out point yet, but I am hoping that happens soon."

"Um . . . ooo-kay." Madden seems all of a sudden to wish he'd chosen another table.

"Do you have dreams, Madden? Do robots dream? Tell me. I need to know!"

"Would you like me to ask my Roomba?"

"Actually, now that I think about it, that seems like a more apt criterion than the Turing test. I dream, therefore I am."

He sits down next to me. Pulls out his ever-present phone.

"Got Elon Musk on that thing? Maybe he'd have some insight on this. Also, I'd like to visit his factory."

"Really? You'd like to crash a Tesla, too?"

"I was thinking I'd just take the rocket ship."

"You know, Paige . . . you may want to keep that list of strategies."

"What?"

"For your star crush, whatever his name is?"

"Really? Why? Oh my God, is my new spy partner Gael García Bernal? Please. Please tell me he and I will fall in love on a boat crossing the Bosphorus in Istanbul. It will be cold with the breeze, but he will lend me his coat and comfort me!"

"Patience, oh delusional one."

8

Everybody gets to be good at something. Need for Speed, from East Los, gets to be good at driving. I get to be good at martial arts. Neither of us gets to be good at carrying a fifty-pound pack over twenty miles through the mud.

This is evidenced by the fact that everyone else is in front of us and, yes, I am the very last one in the pack. Paige Nolan. Last.

Behind me, Randall is barking orders. If you're wondering who Randall is, he's the very large, usually quite warm, African-American training agent who is putting me through my own particular version of hell and humiliation over here. On any other day, I like Randall. Today, I want to strangle Randall.

"What's wrong, Nolan? Didn't eat enough kale today?!"

That is a joke.

Humor.

I would laugh, except I am about to keel over into a pile of mud, sweat, and tears.

"Not easy, is it, Bryn Mawr? You wanna quit?!"

"No, sir."

"What was that?!"

"NO, SIR! I DO NOT WANT TO QUIT, SIR!"

God, this sucks. Why am I even doing this? There's about a mile to go, but I don't think I can make it. It's over a hundred degrees and I'm pretty sure the humidity is making it over a thousand. This is life on Mars during the daytime. This is the fifth circle of hell. This is Oklahoma.

I didn't realize you could sweat from your eye sockets.

The more you know.

One of my legs stops working. I mean, I raise it. That's the first part of a step. I learned that at one. But then, when it comes down it just sort of disappears under me, and now I *timber* headfirst into the mud.

I don't know if you know what it's like to fall flat, face-down in the mud. It's not like any other experience I can describe. It's like the world wallops you in the face in a moment of pain, yes, but the sting of total humiliation is really what gets you. It doesn't get any lower than this. And you can taste it. The mud. Because your face is buried in it. You're literally eating dirt.

Jesus, Mary, and Joseph.

And all the saints.

I can't do this.

Somewhere, behind my head, I can hear Randall barking more insults, but that is just sound and fury signifying nothing.

Because I am not getting up. There's no way.

I'm done.

Look, it was a good run and I gave it the old college try.

Over.

Fin.

But then I hear it. The sound of my mother, from the dream. The screaming. The machine guns lifted up into the air. My mom is screaming for my father. And the guns go off. And I hear the shot.

And now I'm up and running.

That shot is like a starter gun.

And Randall is long behind me.

And I will not let them go gently into the night.

I will rage against the dying of the light.

9

"Sean Raynes? Sean fucking Raynes?!"

Madden waited until we left the industrial cafeteria to spring it on me. I guess he didn't want me to make a scene. We are currently in a sort of default office. At least I hope it's default. I think that chair's from OfficeMax.

"Affirmative."

"You want me to find Sean Raynes and tell you guys where he is. You know that's ridiculous, right? Like, that makes no sense."

"It makes perfect sense."

Madden remains annoyingly expressionless.

"Okay, you do know that this is a guy I worship, right?"

"Like Gael whatever his name is?"

"No, more than that. Like worship/respect. Not worship and want to have five kids with after many years of traveling the world and having steamy nights everywhere from Cinque Terre to Kyoto. This is like *admiration* love."

"Well, then this should be no problem for you."

"No, no, no, no . . . you don't understand. This is like the equivalent of a soap opera. This is like . . . 'Next week on *Eagle's Crest* . . . will Priscilla Von Prissington become a pauper or will she inherit her family estate by murdering her long-lost, slightly deranged, identical twin sister whom she worships but is also slightly jealous of?'"

He grimaces. "What is it like to live inside there?"

"Where?"

"That weird little world between those two ears?"

"What? No, look, stop trying to change the subject. I am not doing this. Okay? No. The answer is no. N. O."

We settle into a kind of warm silence. He's not angry. I think he probably knew this was coming. I decide to take this little break to observe his de facto office, which is much more Zen than I pictured. Minimalist, almost. There's no ornate mahogany desk adorned with paperweights and duck decoys, or a regal bird-patterned wingback chair where I could imagine him reading *The Red Badge of Courage* like a patriotic yet intellectual patriarch as he tasked his underlings.

Nope. There's just a utilitarian gray desk, a phenomenally functional black pleather office chair, and a white coffee mug with some open sugar packets scattered around it.

Funny, I wouldn't have taken him for a sugar guy.

"You know, you really should have some kind of vaguely amusing nonoffensive phrase on your coffee mug."

"Really?"

"Yes."

"Like what?"

"Like . . . 'Keep on truckin'!' or 'Don't let the turkeys get you down!' or maybe a cat dangling from a tree limb—'Hang in there!'"

"Sorry to disappoint."

There's not even a window in here for me to look out of contemplatively.

"I'm not doing this," I tell him finally.

"What?"

"Killing Sean Raynes."

"Whoa. Nobody said anything about *killing* anybody. That's not what this is. Look, Paige, there's been some chatter. A lot of it, actually. He's got something."

"Like what?"

"Like additional intelligence. A fail-safe. Something a lot of people want to get their hands on. Something that could put him in danger. It's part of your job to find out exactly what it is."

"I still don't get it. Why *me*? You have a zillion agents better suited for this."

"Actually, no. We have one. Paige Nolan."

"Okay, sidebar. What does this even have to do with my parents? That's what I'm here for, remember? Not to just do random acts of international traitor wrangling."

"I can assure you, this is no random act."

"Okay, well, what does it have to do with my parents?"

"I'm afraid that's above your pay grade."

"Seriously. Tell me."

"Paige, this is the deal. We can't tell every single agent every single piece of information. You'd all be killed. Or tortured. Or both. It's standard operating procedure to maintain *plausible deniability*, and I need you to just trust me, okay?"

"So, to clarify: You're a government agent. Asking me to trust you."

"Yes."

"Do you have some levees to sell me in New Orleans?"

He sighs. "Paige. This is just a simple fact-finding mission."

"But. You've. Seen. My. Twitter. Page. I know everything about this guy. If there were a fan club, yours truly would be president. Also, possibly the treasurer. You even brought it up in our fake interview."

He's silent. Piercing blue eyes staring directly into mine.

Annnnnnnd, I get it now.

"And that is what makes me the best candidate for this particular operation."

He smiles, pleased that his pupil has mastered this particular lesson, and hands me a folder.

"Here."

I take the folder but whine, "Ugh! This is ridiculous."

"No, this is Liberty's first assignment."

"Who's Liberty?"

"You. It's your code name. I thought you'd like it because it's so . . . patriotic."

"Very amusing."

"But seriously, you have to get me something valuable to bargain with."

"Wait? What do you mean?"

"There are no guarantees, but if you complete the mission successfully, I can get your parents' case made active again."

This room is too drab and horrible for my parents' names to be invoked. Their names should never be uttered in this gray place of afternoons measured out in coffee spoons.

I want to grab this metal desk and throw it at the sky.

"So Liberty, aka me, is going to just waltz into Russia, find Raynes, and—I don't know— chloroform him or something?"

"Of course not."

"Good."

He smirks. "We almost never use chloroform anymore."

10

I guess the general idea here is that I am a foreign exchange student. At Moscow State University. Which is like the Harvard of Russia. So I'm a *smart* foreign exchange student. Honestly, I think they could do better. Why not make me a chef or an acrobat or something with a little more zing and zest? I mean, I guess the strong suit around here isn't the creative department.

I really shouldn't be surprised that the seat next to me in *coach* class on my way over to Moscow, which was heretofore vacant, is suddenly filled with a certain conservative-yet-not-horribly-unattractive-looking someone named Madden.

He plops down next to me.

Just as I was enjoying my second vodka tonic.

"It's really embarrassing how you keep following me."

He smirks.

"In the words of Aerosmith: dream on."

"You know that guy's like a hundred and three, right?"

"Which guy?"

"You know, the mouth guy."

"Are you talking about Steven Tyler?"

"Maybe. I'm actually not sure."

The flight attendant passes and smiles at Madden for just a second too long.

"Gag. She's flirting with you. Are you in first?"

"Of course."

"Capitalist. So, to what do I owe the honor of this visit to steerage?"

"I'd like you to take a look at this."

"Is it your penis?"

He slouches, sighs. "Why are you so annoying?"

"Nobody knows. It's one of the great mysteries of the world, like who built the pyramids, or why is the Trader Joe's parking lot always so squirrelly, or why is Donald Trump orange?"

"Here. Take a look."

He shows me an old-fashioned photograph. I don't mean a black-and-white photograph. I mean, it's old-fashioned.

Because it's a photograph. Printed on actual paper. From a tree.

"This is very high-tech of you."

He shakes his head in an almost imperceptible display of disappointment. "Analog. Unhackable."

Ah.

"Now I'm going to give you this, you're going to memorize this face, and then you're going to burn the picture. Please wait until we've landed."

There in the picture is a textbook villain staring back at me. Well, not at me, exactly, as the image seems to be taken from security camera footage much higher than eye level. But whoever he's staring at, looks like he best watch the hell out. He has black hair, a black jacket, and, clearly, a black heart.

"Whoa. Are you sure you didn't find this guy in central casting?"

We stare at this photograph. A collective shudder goes through us. Honestly, this guy looks like he'd slit your throat for a quarter.

"Oleg Zamiatin," says Madden.

"I never thought I'd say this, but he looks like an Oleg."

"He's one of Russia's most decorated Spetsnaz commandos—"

"Spetsnaz?"

"Their version of the SEALs. He's a former Olympic judo champion and sometime assassin, and will likely be Raynes's last line of defense if you manage to separate him from the other FSB agents."

"So you're basically showing me a picture of the guy who's going to kill me."

"No, I'm showing you a picture of the guy you will be dealing with and might have to, worst-case scenario, fight. Possibly. In self-defense."

"Cool. That's cool. Can I go home now?"

"Remember, Paige, *all you're doing is finding out what Raynes has.* You're fine. You've got this."

In case you were wondering, FSB is the Federal Security Service of the Russian Federation. I know what you're thinking. Shouldn't it be *Bureau* since it's *FSB*? But it's the Russian alphabet. Cyrillic script. Things get wonky between alphabets.

Here's what is clear: the Soviet-era KGB is now basically the FSB. It's a branding thing. Like if Halliburton one day was like, *Hey, everybody hates us. Let's change our name to Palliburton!*

Same shit, different color.

"The FSB are protecting him."

"Because he's basically a national embarrassment to the United States, and they love that."

"Exactly. And . . . they don't know what additional intelligence he has either. Just like us, whatever it is, they want it."

"Guess he was smart to go to Russia."

"He didn't *choose* to go to Russia," Madden snaps. "We revoked his passport over Russian airspace. He had no choice!"

"Oh, *that* was nice of you."

"Yeah, well. It worked. Even the brilliant Paige Nolan thinks he *chose* to go to Russia. And to some people, that makes Raynes a traitor." He pauses. "I have to admit. I can't believe we fooled you."

"Hopefully, that will be the last time."

We sit there for a moment in awkward silence.

"Why did you snap just now?"

"What?"

"You kind of jumped down my throat just then. To be honest."

Madden is somewhere else.

"I have no idea what you're talking about."

He gets up and goes back to first class.

And there I sit, looking after him. O-kaaaay. That was a Dr. Jekyll-and-Mr. Hyde moment.

Is it possible Madden is more complicated than I thought? Maybe there is something more to him than his buttoned-up facade . . .

I look down at the picture of Darth Oleg.

"It's okay. It's totally fine. I've got this."

This is my way of making myself feel better.

Oh, and . . .

It's totally not working.

11

Wow. I wasn't prepared for how cool all the girls would dress over here. Like, not at all.

Moscow is like Paris meets Tokyo. And it is off the charts.

TV shows in America would have you believe in dumb stereotypes. Like every lady here should be platinum blond with a fur coat and sparkly jewelry. No, no. These women are dressed with a studied nonchalance and what I've heard people on *Project Runway* refer to as "a sense of play." I've been off the plane now, walking around, for four hours, and I already have ten different outfits I'm planning to imitate.

And that's not all. These girls over here, these ladies . . . are seriously strutting it up. There is no apology, no self-deprecation. It is just a full-court runway walk down the street, over cobblestones, in five-inch heels. This is normal: running in stilettos, over stone-paved streets, looking like you are a page out of *Vogue* somehow animated. This is a thing.

Also, there is this shocking truth. This *city*. Moscow. It's a lot more . . . enchanting than I would have ever imagined. I mean, doesn't everyone joke that everything here is ugly and drab? Nothing but gray and bread lines and propaganda? Not so . . . There are shiny silver skyscrapers splicing the air behind a backdrop of the Kremlin and about a hundred other majestic buildings that seem like something Walt Disney might want to re-create at Disneyland. *And over here, folks, the Kremlin Teacups! Step right up to the Red Square Roller Coaster of Doom! Ladies and gentlemen, free borscht with your funnel cakes!*

Turn around, look in every direction, and you will see the Byzantine, onion-shaped domes of whatever superfantastic thousand-year-old Russian Orthodox church happens to just be there. In colors of blue, red, sienna, gold, turquoise. Turquoise! Or let's try the Baroque palaces, shall we? Houses, buildings, museums . . . painted pink, sky blue, yellow, lime green, with bright-white molding around the windows, doors, and columns. In New York, any one of these buildings would be on the Visitors' Guide. Here: Oh, they just happen to be there; who even knows what they are? Now let's look over there: an imposing Soviet-era building with "CCCP" etched at the top, harkening back to the horrible old days, which really weren't that long ago, honestly. This is what I can't help but think, walking passed a "Soviet-era kitsch café" with a hammer and sickle on the menu, ironically. Ironically!

Seriously, what is this place?

To make matters even more bizarre, forget about your old, dumb alphabet. Here everything is in the Cyrillic alphabet, so look alive. Just remember, "restaurant" is spelled "pectopah." That should help.

Fun fact: Every place plays techno. No, not . . . Oh, they play a lot of techno here. *Every* place. Every restaurant, bar, clothing store, sidewalk café, gas station, dentist, and kindergarten. It's all techno. For real. I don't know when this law was put into decree, but I think it's mandatory.

I am taking this all in as I walk toward the hulking, imposing MSU campus.

Now Moscow State University itself is basically centered around this giant tall building, which was the tallest building in all of Europe until 1990. It's generally elegant, but there's definitely something wrong with the proportions. I'm not sure what exactly. I can't put my finger on it. There are elegant buildings all over the place and a green and rather insanely large gazing pond. If you're in the mood for gazing.

But the elegance ends there.

Just wait until you see the dorm.

"This is Moscow State University dorm. You share entryway, toilet, and shower. There is shared kitchen on each floor, but stay out of refrigerator . . ."

She plugs her nose in the international gesture of *yuck*. My Moscow State University welcoming committee consists of one native Stalin-era babushka walking me through the dorm, which looks like an aesthetic mix of Amish minimalism and bomb-shelter couture. Suddenly, it doesn't matter that I'm a covert spy on foreign land, sent to extract information from the biggest threat to my nation's security. Suddenly, looking at the robin's-egg-blue crumbling paint on the walls, which is most definitely lead, and the mold on the ceiling above me, I think what my mother would do if she saw this. Honestly, it makes me shudder. She would throw herself against me and drag me out of here in a panic. She would practically burst. "Oh my God, this place is full of chemicals, chipping lead paint! Mold spores! And probably asbestos." She would have me out the door in two seconds flat.

"How are the bugs? . . . *Kak yavlyayutsya oshibki?*" I ask.

She looks at me. I can tell she's weighing whether to tell me the truth. I spoke Russian, so she doesn't take me as completely horrible.

She goes with a so-so hand gesture and a squiggly mouthed smile.

Welp, good thing I brought my 100-percent-organic bug-killing hotels.

"How are the mice? Any mice? . . . *Kak myshey? Lyubyye myshey?*"

Same gesture.

Welp, good thing I brought my 100-percent-organic mouse-removal hotels.

She gives me a shrug and a smile. What can you do? Now she's off to introduce some other poor American to the true wonders and slow poisoning of a Moscow dorm room.

I'm okay, though. I'm going to be okay.

When we flew over Moscow before we landed, I had this feeling like I was on a Tilt-A-Whirl, reeling through some kind of carnival, and there was really no hope in all of this, and I was an idiot.

I mean, this chance at getting my parents back? This isn't real. This was just some strange dream I am having, and soon I will wake up back at Bryn Mawr, next to one of my three trusty hookups and all will be well. I will gather my clothes and tiptoe out of one of their bedrooms before having to make awkward breakfast conversation.

You know. Like a *normal person.*

Sidebar: I really don't understand how anyone could actually have breakfast with someone they just slept with. Like, what are you supposed to even say? *Hey, remember that part with your tongue last night? Well. I really liked that. Good job.* I mean, seriously. It's just so much easier to gather your boots and get the hell out of Dodge. I always feel a panic in that moment. Like . . . *please don't wake up please don't wake up please don't wake up.* The horror of crouching over my clothes, half-naked, and having to make small talk, overrides all my usual brain function. This fear has left me to abandon more than one pair of underwear in a fit of panic.

But in that moment just before landing, looking out on Red Square and the skyscrapers in the distance, I would take that awkward, half-naked crouching conversation any day of the week. What the hell am I doing? Who exactly do I think I am?

But then I remember my mom and the organic spaz attack she would have over the chemically toxic dorm room.

It reminds me why I'm here.

Once she changed all the mattresses in the house in a random freak-out about flame retardants and off-gassing. One other time she threw out everything under the sink, staring at the backs of the cleaning supplies, squinting at the labels, saying, "Oh Jesus," and then hurling them each into the trash. My dad would just stand there watching her, slightly bemused. God, he loved—

Loves her.

Right? *Loves* her. Because that is what all of this is for, that present tense. They are alive and he loves her *currently* and I love them *still*.

We were in Bethlehem, Palestine, once, when my dad was doing a story about an art school there, a school started by a young boy from a refugee camp. It was an inspiring story. A story of hope in the midst of chaos. Total Pulitzer contender. We went to see the artwork of the students, the oldest of whom were seventeen. The youngest student was five—a little girl who had wandered into the school and literally just picked up a brush.

My mom was talking to the little girl, asking about her painting. "Who is this? And who is that? And what are they doing?" The little girl was smiling, a little bit shy, but after a while she warmed up to my mom. And she was standing there, almost under her wing, looking up with a smile on her face. This tiny little girl from Bethlehem with big brown eyes. She kept wrapping her little fingers around my mom's necklace. Some crazy thing she had bought on the streets of Istanbul.

And my mom noticed she kept grabbing the necklace, dazzled by it and fascinated by it, too. A ludicrous mix of colors and ribbons and stones. Large embroidery thread. It made no sense, in a way, the necklace. But I remember looking over and seeing my mom take off the necklace and give it to the little girl. I remember the little girl, her eyes lighting up. She couldn't believe it. It was like giving her a ship of gold.

And the little girl hugs my mom close, like she's known her her whole life, like she was an aunt or a cousin or a sister.

And I see my mom's face over the little girl's shoulder. A tear in her eye.

And I know why she's crying. She's crying because she wishes she could do more. Because she feels helpless. And all she wants to do is help this little girl. Give her a better life. A life free of violence.

And my father sees my mother, too. And he looks at me.

We share a moment.

In that moment, that is all we wish to be.

My mother.

Present tense.

She's alive.

And my father's alive.

And I will save them.

As if in response, a tiny gray mouse scurries across the bed frame.

That's okay, mouse. You're part of the plan, too.

It appears my roommate's yet to arrive, so I get to lay claim to the bed of my choosing. Do I want the bed next to the crumbling lead paint that will probably fall into my mouth while I'm sleeping or the bed next to the dilapidated heater that will inevitably start a fire at three in the morning?

Heater it is.

12

Remember when I told you how the girls here dress super-cool and may possibly be the coolest-dressing girls on Earth? Welp, that is confirmed when I see her. My roommate.

There she stands, framed by the doorway.

There are a lot of things I would like to say to this girl. A thousand things. But my tongue is tied by the fact that she is wearing a jacket I want to immediately steal from her body.

Let me describe it to you. It won't make sense. In fact, it will probably sound ugly. But it's not. Oh, Lord above. It. Is. Not.

This jacket is sort of a mustard beige color, and it's a trench, tied at the waist over the double row of buttons. But that's not what's going on here. Here's what's going on . . .

The top of this mustard trench is like an alien made a necklace-slash-collar out of weird alien stones. Peach, royal blue, light blue, dark peach, beige, and black. In squares and triangles.

I know.

It sounds hideous.

But it is the coolest item of clothing I think I have ever seen. Like she found it for nothing from a street vendor somewhere ludicrously remote or possibly it's couture and costs a million dollars.

But wait, there's more!

Her hair. Okay. Her hair. It's dark brown at the top, almost black. Then there are sharp bangs, right across her forehead, then the dark hair turns kind of light, then it turns like a pale shade of beige. Not blond, mind you. Oh, no. Almost like taupe. And then the whole thing ends just below her shoulders.

WTF.

I guess I didn't realize I would be rooming with the late David Bowie's young female Russian equivalent. Jesus Christ. I look down at my "#arrestCheney" T-shirt and wish I had put a little more effort into my entire ensemble

She smiles. "This shirt. I like."

So she appreciates my "#arrestCheney" T-shirt. Okay. Okay, that's good. We are off to a good start.

"I see you put me next to lead paint."

She gestures toward the vacant, toxic twin bed.

"I thought maybe Russians, like, drank that stuff for breakfast or something."

"You are funny girl. I kill you last."

Silence.

And now she breaks out in a laugh. A thick bark of a laugh that welcomes me to this place somehow.

"Here." She pulls out a bottle. "Georgian vodka. We drink."

Well, folks, when you just land in Russia and Ziggy Stardust's body double tells you *we drink*, then we drink.

That's just etiquette.

And my mother raised me to always be polite.

13

Her name is Katerina, of course. Katerina Markova.

And this is how we drink.

Katerina leads me through the streets of Moscow, past Manege Square and Gorky Park, we end up in front of a completely nondescript building at the end of a long alley.

She pushes a cold metal number on a list and the gray door buzzes open. Now there's a flight of cinder-block stairs. At the first landing, a girl scurries past us, dressed in thigh-high stockings and a white peacoat buttoned up to her chin, *avec* epaulets. She ignores us except for a slight flip of her burgundy bob. I follow Katerina, a few steps behind, as she reaches a door slightly ajar.

Katerina gives me a quick backward look, a Cheshire cat

grin, and opens the door.

And now I know why she gave me that grin.

Outside it's gray and bland and lifeless. But opening the door to this place, this secret place, it's like she's opening the door to a Technicolor wonderland of hipster utopia. Where everyone looks like they're from either Echo Park or Williamsburg or Oberkampf. You could point the camera in any direction and that would be your album cover.

There are pink-and-gold cigarettes tucked in purses, bouffants, oversized sweaters, suspenders, ironic mustaches, skinny boys who look like they just fell out of bed and, now . . . us. I'm expecting a cool reception, because this seems to be the epicenter of *haute* in the universe.

But no.

This is Katerina's place.

She takes a seat at the end of a long table, lit by candlelight, with the walls painted green around us and art everywhere, real art, from real people, probably who are sitting here at this table right this very second. This is a long table, by the way. There are about twenty people at this table. And there are other tables, too. But from the looks of it, this is THE table. And, from the looks of everyone, Katerina is the person to be with.

Okay, I can handle that. I just landed four hours ago, but it's cool.

"Secret supper club," she offers, as explanation. "Came out of iron curtain. We have to do fun things as secret."

Behind her, there is a giant mirror with a gold gilded frame. I steal a glance at myself in the mirror and hope I measure up. I'm pretty sure I don't.

"Now let's find out why you are here," she proclaims.

She's pouring my third shot of vodka already, but who's counting? These people drink. I'm not kidding. Like they REALLY. FUCKING. DRINK.

Katerina smiles, that Cheshire cat smile again.

"Now American Paige. Are you spy?"

14

There's about five hundred different things going through my mind. Five hundred different possible answers I could give. It's like one of those Choose Your Own Adventure books: Answer A, turn to page 137, and get sent into a dark cave to be eaten by a bear. Answer B, turn to page 5, and find yourself at the business end of a Kalashnikov. (For those of you not in the spy game, a Kalashnikov is like a Russian Uzi. Thanks, paramilitary training!)

I am just about to attempt a response when a very thin, dark-haired boy in a hoodie comes sidling up beside Katerina. He has dark purple circles under his eyes, but there's something attractive about him. Something simultaneously puppylike and sleepy. And harmless. And a little pathetic. Like a Slavic Bieber.

He stares at us.

I stare back.

"Yes. I know you are dying for me to introduce myself, so I won't make you wait any longer."

I'm expecting Katerina to send this guy packing, but she continues to gaze placidly at him. I really have no idea why.

"You like club? You like hip-hop? You want beatbox?"

There's an extremely awkward silence as I study my vodka and Katerina says nothing.

"I think he is asking *you*, American Paige."

"Ahhh! You are American! No wonder you are so stuck-up and spoiled!"

I turn to Katerina. My eyes are all, *Is he serious right now?*

Katerina attempts an explanation. "Usually, in Moscow, if someone, a man, comes up to you and begins talking to you . . . you are supposed to answer him."

"Really? But I don't even know him."

"It is just different culture."

"What if he's a rapist?"

She gestures in his direction. "Look at him!" She laughs. "He is not rapist."

"Hello? I am right here. You can see?" He gestures to himself.

I lean in to Katerina.

"I don't understand this. I'm just supposed to talk to any and every random guy who comes up to me? And, like, be nice?"

Katerina smiles. "Yes."

"*Any* guy? Like even ones with, like, extra limbs or whatever?"

"Yes."

I sigh.

"Okay. I'm going to talk to you now. I wasn't trying to be rude or anything. It's just . . . in the States we don't randomly talk to any guy. Because *serial killers*. However, to answer your question . . . I do like club. I do like hip-hop. Not sure about beatbox . . . but I appreciate the effort."

"I love Young Jeezy! He is also American!"

"Okay, yes. But I'm not, like, *him* or anything."

"You are American like him. He is best!"

Katerina is looking at me with amusement.

"Is it horrible for you?"

"What?"

"Talking to stranger?"

"If I'm going to be honest, yes. I'm uncomfortable. This is not my strong suit. Even back home. But since you're here. And we're in a double-secret supper club. I am making an effort."

"I am Uri," the boy tells me. "Uri Usoyan. And you are?"

"Katerina."

He nods. "Nice to meet you, Katerina. And you? What is American girl's name?"

"Paige."

"Paige. Like page in book?"

"Yes. Like page in book."

"Maybe one day, Uri will read you." He smiles.

Ew.

"I don't really know what that means exactly, but I'm trying not to be 'unapproachable, spoiled American girl,' so now *I* will smile. Also, I just said that out loud."

Katerina laughs.

"Here. More vodka."

She pours me what must be my fifth shot and pats me on the back.

"Don't worry. I won't leave you in street."

Uri turns back to me. "I'd like you to meet my friend, someone very close to me. It is . . . my penis."

I spit the drink halfway across the room. "What? Oh. My. God!"

Katerina lets out a laugh.

Uri gives me a wink. "It is joke. You see, harmless? I'll find you later, nerd American dork. I always find cute girl."

He saunters off.

"You like him?"

"Um. I sort of don't know what just happened."

"But you like?"

"He's not really my type. Kind of smarmy, actually . . ."

"What is smarmy?"

"Proud of himself. And slick."

"Ah! Well, that is why because he happens to be son of Moscow's most notorious gangster."

"Are you serious?"

"See? I told you you should be more careful who you talk to."

She winks and I do what can only be described as a drunken swat of playfulness.

And hover there a moment, then collapse in a heap on the table.

Stupid vodka.

15

I have to tell you something.

Now before I tell this to you, let me just explain . . . I don't know any of this is happening in this moment. I find out later.

But I'm gonna tell it to you, right here and now, because this is really when it's actually happening. And I'm gonna tell this to you so you realize just how absolutely screwed I am right now and just how in over my head I am. Because it's really something.

Now what I'm sharing with you is another videotape. Actually, I'll be sharing a bunch of them. So just be prepared. I'm not going to tell you where I got them, or when, because that would spoil all the fun, now, wouldn't it?

Just watch.

Observe.

Laugh at my expense.

Truly.

Because if I had known any of this was going on, well, I'd be on the first plane home back to Philly.

So, without further ado, come with me now . . . into this videotape!

I know, I know. Just follow me and don't make too much noise. I don't want them to hear you.

What we are looking at right now, you and I, is a very, and I mean *very* fancy restaurant in Moscow. This is, like, where Vladimir Putin has his lunch, when he's not bare-chested fishing, bare-chested invading neighboring countries, or bare-chested posing for calendars. Yes, there is a sexy Putin calendar. January through December, lots of man boobs, lots of outdoor activity. I've been dying to get my hands on one since I heard about it. I want to display it in my room. You know, ironically. But get this. They are sold out.

Anyway, back to the video. We are perched somewhere in the ceiling. I imagine we are looking at this from a chandelier. Who knows what the camera looks like? Whatever it is, it must be small, because we are basically right on top of this table.

If there weren't a very large bald man with slightly tinted

glasses sitting at this table, you would have thought we went back in time. To the Baroque period. Every inch of the ceiling, every inch of the walls, around the doors, around the windows, around the fireplace is covered in either white, light blue, gold, or a kind of vaguely Asian mural. It basically looks like, at any moment, Marie Antoinette is going to come strutting in the room proclaiming, "Let them eat cake!"

I'm not going to lie to you. I wish I could live in this room. It's insane and overly done and embellished and gilded and everything I would never think I would like because I pride myself on *not* being a fetishistic consumer—but it is stunning. Yes, I want to live here. With Gael García Bernal. My figmental boyfriend.

But right now the person who is living here, or who is dining here, is a rather portly, not-very-nice-looking, hair-challenged man in glasses, who I will introduce to you. Don't look him in the eye. Just kidding. We're watching videotape, remember? He can't see you.

This man, sitting below us, unbeknownst to us spying on him, is none other than Dimitri Kolya Usoyan. Basically, the John Gotti of Moscow.

If you don't know who John Gotti is, I'll give you a chance to Google.

There.

Are you back?

Okay, good. Try to stick with me here.

So, remember that kind-of-cheesy guy who came up and just started randomly talking to me at the secret supper club last night? The one who I was supposed to talk to because I guess girls here are supposed to talk to every Tom, Dick, and Vlad who comes out of the woodwork? Well, that kid, Uri, is this guy's son. And this guy, Dimitri, the one we are looking at, looks like he could wrestle a bear. And win.

Now watch with me for a second.

Beside him sits a kind of ice princess with white-blond hair, who is completely disinterested in everything around her and who has been checking her lipstick in a knife for the past hour. For obvious reasons we'll call her Elsa. And on the other side of Dimitri is a man in a dark blazer who sits down. Judging by his fidgeting hands, he's some kind of minion. Let's just call him Underling.

"Why the long wait?"

"There is FSB everywhere. Oleg is like mommy to him. Will not let him out of sight." Underling seems a bit nervous.

"What about noise?"

"Yes, there is chatter. We don't know. We are trying to figure out."

"You have billion-dollar baby just sitting there drinking

his latte and you do nothing?" Dimitri smiles at Underling. It's not a nice smile. It's more like a kill-you smile.

"Everybody know he is like billion-dollar baby. That is why Oleg is man for job. He must have twenty FSB agents, all around. Is like Putin's personal guard."

"Never mind. We will find a way. In the meantime, find me more bidders."

"How to find bidders when we don't know what they are bidding for?"

"You try to say freedom hacker, with number one clearance, does not have valuable information up sleeve? He must have. Or CIA kill him by now. You try to say States just happy to have him floating around? Making them look like no-pants embarrassment?"

Underling shakes his head. "Americans—very uptight about nudity."

"Get me more bidders. Or I get Raynes myself."

And with that, bald, pudgy, and mean stands up with his blasé Queen Elsa and the two of them glide out of this palatial insanity, presumably leaving Underling with the bill.

So, there you have it. Now you know. RAITH is not the only one interested in Raynes.

To recap: Sean Raynes is a "person of interest" to us, the Russians, and this guy, Dimitri, aka Moscow Kingpin, who does not qualify as the Russian government but as more of a—what do you call it—a *freelancer.*

The question is . . . how long can Raynes remain a "person of interest" before he inevitably becomes a "person who is six feet under"?

And why is he not dead already?

Questions to ponder. But let's get back to our regularly scheduled programming, shall we?

16

Congratulations.

You made it to the first day of my mission.

Operation Make Raynes Notice Me begins this morning. Look, no offense, but I just need you to stay in the background for this part. Otherwise, you could blow it.

You'll be happy to know I did a little bit of research on Sean Raynes and I have found that we actually do have something in common.

We both share a love of Elliott Smith.

If you don't know who Elliott Smith is, let me enlighten you. Imagine the most beautiful but sad lyrics set to the most beautiful but sad guitar sung by the most troubled person in the history of mankind. Then imagine that troubled, beautiful, and sad person kills himself and all of the beautiful and sad music he was ever going to make for the rest of his life is gone forever. But he left us the music he made before.

That's Elliott Smith.

Don't worry. When you listen to him you'll understand.

Now it turns out that Sean Raynes, *the* Sean Raynes, who everybody and their dog is either spying on, plotting against, or sending naked pics to (That last part is true, by the way. He had to tweet everybody to stop sending him naked pictures of themselves.) also, like yours truly, has a love of the profound emo kick in the teeth that is Elliott Smith.

So my plan of attack is as follows:

First, I will wear my Elliott Smith T-shirt, which does not say "Elliott Smith" because that is way too on the nose and commercial but says, instead, "SAY YES." This happens to be a name of one of his songs. That is all. Just "SAY YES" on a black background in cursive-y disturbed letters.

Second, I will venture to Café Treplev, which is a hidden, wooden, book-lined restaurant that looks more like someone's personal library than a place of commerce. It, in fact, looks like the library I would like to one day have in my imaginary mansion on the cliff with Gael. Oh, you don't have an imaginary mansion on the cliff? Fine. You can come over to mine. But don't steal the soaps.

Madden has done me the kind favor of equipping me with all of Raynes's routines and his most frequented stop is this little precious gem because Raynes is cool and, also, he is obviously trying to lay low, what with all the people trying to find him, shake him down, kill him, and send him the aforementioned naked photos.

If you're wondering where I am in this little nook, I am in an actual nook in the corner. A book nook. I am wearing my "SAY YES" T-shirt and I am pretending to be calm, cool, collected, and definitely not stalking anyone.

Except . . . there he is.

Oh, sweet Jesus.

I really wasn't expecting him to show up for another hour or so. I guess Madden's research is out-of-date.

There he is, Sean Raynes, in all his glasses-wearing, raven-haired, skinny-but-sexy-AF glory. His hair's a little messy and he probably didn't shave for the past two days, but that is just adding to the effect.

It is possible there may be live ladybugs in my stomach.

I am not kidding. They are in there, and I think they are mating.

America's number one most polarizing enemy of the state walks to the counter and orders an espresso.

Behind him, and probably all around him, are very calm-looking gentlemen of the kind that could obviously kill you because everyone in this entire café is probably an FSB agent. I do not see Oleg. I guess he is maniacally petting a cat somewhere.

Now America's number one enemy is waiting for his espresso.

And now . . .

America's number one enemy is looking at my T-shirt.

I pretend, without turning beet red, that I am still reading my book, which is *White Noise* by Don DeLillo. (An excellent book, which I recommend to anyone interested, and which I have chosen because it seems intellectual enough to imply intelligence but not pretentious enough to seem contrived. Like, if I were reading *War and Peace* . . . too obvious.)

I can tell, using my spider sense, that he is now investigating the girl wrapped in the "SAY YES" T-shirt. Aka, me.

Pale. Check. Mouse-brown hair. Check. Reading a cool, intellectual but not too pretentious book in English. Check.

And this magic moment could last forever. In fact, I wish it would. There is *something* to being checked out by America's most polarizing figure that is most definitely, and unexpectedly, hot.

Except that now some doofus jumps out in front of Raynes and snaps a picture with his iPhone. And now that doofus is grabbed by the arm and flung into a table, and his phone is smashed by a hearty but diabolical-looking man who is most definitely Oleg Zamiatin.

Ah, Oleg. Nice of you to join us! First-time caller, long-time fan.

The doofus lies there recovering on the parquet floor while Sean Raynes, who I will now call America's Hottest Enemy Number One, is whisked out by all the seemingly normal people of the café who were FSB agents all along. Wow. There are a lot of them. Even one of the cashiers!

Raynes is practically carried out with his feet off the ground but right before he clears the doorway, and I mean this by millimeters . . .

He. Looks. Back.

At me.

17

When I get back to my dorm room, there it is, staring at me from above my bed. The Vladimir Putin calendar. Ha! I guess Katerina got a copy of it for me after my drunken rant at the secret supper club about how I had to ironically have one.

This is a girl after my own heart.

You have to see this calendar.

July: Vladimir Putin fly-fishing topless. March: Vladimir Putin smelling a flower. November: Vladimir Putin holding a puppy. I'm not kidding. *Holding a puppy!*

I laugh to myself. Katerina sure has my number. Maybe she will be my BFF even after I go back to the States.

Wait. Do I have a new friend?

Or, really, *a* friend?

There's a pair of red Beats in my suitcase. You know, the Dr. Dre headphones everyone's crazy about. And I am crazy about them, too. The only problem is . . . I don't own any red Beats. So, that's interesting.

I pick them up and inspect them.

Underneath, there's a note: *For you, Bryn Mawr.*

Hmm.

I put them on and immediately hear Madden.

"Go outside. Now."

Ah. I get it. Subterfugeian communication device. Clever.

It's not far to the Moskva River, so I suppose I could just pretend to jog along the river. While I listen to my spy overlord.

"What do you know about your roommate? Just talk. I can hear you."

"She's cool. She's beautiful. She got me a Vladimir Putin calendar to masturbate to." I swear I can *hear* Madden blush.

"Do you think she's FSB?"

"Not sure. She certainly *looks* cool enough to be a spy."

"What about this Uri guy? The guy from the secret supper club."

"Are you serious right now? How do you know about Uri?"

"Oh, did I forget to tell you your purse is bugged? And

there's a camera involved. By the way, you really can't hold your liquor, Bryn Mawr. We've got something to help with that. I'll get you some."

"Thanks. Did you see Raynes this morning, then?"

"Yes, we did. Nicely done. Wait two days before going back. You don't want to seem desperate."

"Uh, thanks, *girlfriend*, for your *sisterly* advice. By the way, loving my shitty digs."

"Think of it as having an authentic experience. Look, keep an eye on that Uri. Get close. Fit in. Not that you could ever fit in anywhere."

"Aw! Does that mean you're not going to take me home to meet your mother?"

"Paige, you may be surprised to hear this, but my mother would actually love you."

"Really?"

"Yes. She's a sucker for lost causes. Night-night."

And *click*, there he goes, Madden and my connection to the States. This may sound pathetic, but I might miss it in a few days. That's the funny thing. I consider myself to be so worldly, but then whenever I go anywhere, I start getting homesick after about four days. Totally pathetic.

I guess I'll have to find some kind of faux-American café and order a grilled cheese and french fries. But not yet. I'll hold out. I should at least wait a week otherwise I won't respect myself in the morning.

The sun is starting to set over the Moskva River, bright-pink-and-blue clouds. A white river cruise boat floats by under the bridge. I have to admit, I wasn't prepared for the beauty of this city. Venice? Yes. Kyoto? Of course. But Moscow? Honestly, who knew?

I'm not halfway back to campus when I see Katerina.

"Ah, you are jogging. Healthy, American girl."

"It's honestly unfair that I'm the one jogging and you're the one who's so skinny, but I'm trying not to focus on that right now."

She smiles.

"You like calendar?"

"I love calendar," I tell her. It's possible that actual hearts are dancing in my eyes when I say it.

"We have invite tonight, yes?"

We are walking past the gazing pond, back to the dorm. Everywhere around us is the rush of students, that excitement you get at sunset. What's gonna happen? What's gonna happen tonight?

"We have invite? Where do we have invite?"

"To club. From your boyfriend, Uri, gangster boy."

"Should we go?"

Katerina shrugs.

Madden did just ask me to fit in.

"You know what, let's do. Let's go."

"Are you sure? His dad is really no joke. This is Moscow, not Disneyland."

"Katerina, honestly, why do you think he wants to be friends with us so badly?"

"The answer is in your pants."

Once again, I find myself play-swatting my new bae.

"But I am serious, American Paige . . . These places, especially with gangster, it is not like cakewalk. And everyone knows Americans are like little baby with no idea what is going on."

"Yes, I am little baby. Bring me to club. Give me bottle."

Katerina smiles.

"I guess you are adventurous little baby."

I smirk. *"Da."*

18

What do you do when the Cold War is over, kind of, and you are stuck with a bunch of bunkers all over the place?

Well, if you're Russian, I guess you turn one of those bunkers into a club. Which is where we are now. And, by the way, they've really gone full throttle with the kind of Cold War, Stalin, agitprop theme. Everything in here is in that Russian Stalin font, and there are profiles of Lenin everywhere. But it's ironic. I think.

There's an entire back area, complete with its own vodka bar, where Uri sits. You would think there would be more people back here. VIP's so lonely.

Katerina and I are not halfway through the door when he gets up.

"Weeeehhll. American girl. Will you talk to me now?"

"Well, now that I'm properly introduced, I think it's okay."

"Ah, so proper, you Americans, while you are busy robbing the world of its resources."

Can't say I disagree with him.

"But you do it with smile, no?"

He smiles and gestures for Katerina and me to sit.

"Please, Uri, don't bore our new friend with your thoughts on American foreign policy. She is one of the good ones. Stick to rap."

Nice of Katerina to stick up for me. I didn't know I was one of the good ones.

"So, tell me, Paige, why is it you come to Russia?"

"To become a lesbian."

Uri snarfs his drink. "That is funny! You make jokes. I make rhymes."

"Excuse me?"

Suddenly, Uri starts beatboxing in earnest.

"*Yo, I'm not straight out of Compton, I'm straight from the Kremlin, come hop in my Bentley, take a ride with the kingpin.*"

Uri looks to me expectantly.

It really is *always* uncomfortable when anyone starts trying to rap in front of you. Especially if they're white.

"I have to give you credit. It's not that easy to rhyme with

Kremlin. All I can think of, honestly, is *gremlin.*"

"Do you like this club?" He motions around for Katerina and me to be dazzled. "It is like dream from my pants."

"I think something got lost in translation there."

Katerina smiles and orders a vodka. Or rather, a *bottle* of vodka.

This bottle, of course, leads to other bottles and other toasts and more bottles and more toasts . . . and before I know it the top of this bunker-slash-bar is spinning around in Cold War circles.

All part of the job.

Luckily, nothing of note happens.

Except. Well, there is one thing.

At around two in the morning the place erupts in gunfire.

Oh yeah. That.

19

You never really know what you're going to do when a place explodes into a hail of bullets until it happens to you.

I would like to think I would be especially brave, but what happens in this case is that I dive under a table, only to watch as Katerina throws Uri behind her and basically starts shooting back.

So Katerina is packing heat.

Good to know.

I, on the other hand, am not packing heat. I, on the other hand, am being rushed out of this place by Uri's bodyguards, Uri, and pistol-packin' Katerina.

The funny thing about putting a bar in a bunker is that there are actually a million little secret hallways everywhere to hide in, scurry to, or hightail it out of in a blaze of glory. The supersecret hallway we're in is painted bright burgundy and there is a silhouette of the Kremlin with a hammer and sickle underneath. But I am not here to enjoy the totalitarian art.

Uri's bodyguards seem to be holding the back of this brigade, as the three of us rush through a seemingly endless concrete maze, with bullets zinging around in the background. *Pshew. Pshew. Blam. Pshew.*

Have I mentioned that I hate guns?

It seems like we wind and wind farther and farther through this endless vestige of a Cold War fantasy until finally Katerina slams open a door and a rush of biting air flies past us. The Moscow cold slaps us in the face as we are suddenly driven outside.

This would all be perfect except two extremely blond, muscle-bound men appear out of nowhere. It's possible they emerged either out of the alley or a Monster Energy drink sales convention. Not sure.

They stand there for a second.

And then one of them kicks the gun out of Katerina's hand.

Welp, I was trying to preserve my cover, but right now I think I possibly, potentially, might be in actual danger with my new bae and future, never-to-be, rap-star boyfriend.

What to do, what to do . . . ?

"You! Come."

No-neck blond nods to Uri. It's not much of a nod, though. You need a neck to nod. Try it. Without a neck it's more of a spasm.

Katerina and I stand there for a second in what I can only assume are our very own respective interior monologues.

And then . . . I do the oldest trick in the book, which I seriously can't believe they fall for, but, let's face it, we are not dealing with Albert Einstein and Stephen Hawking over here.

I look behind them, point, and yell, "Holy fuckballs!"

When they turn to look, which they do because they have the collective IQ of a stick, I resort to the art of Muay Thai.

Also, in case you're keeping tabs, I start seeing all of this from above me again. These high-stakes moments really do bring out the need to disassociate. It's okay, though. If I get pummeled here the best part is it's not really me. It's that other me. That I happen to be wrapped in.

The thing about Muay Thai is, it's known as the "art of the eight limbs." What that means is . . . even the hard things, like elbows, knees, and shins are involved. As a discipline it's basically a bone crusher, and it's not for the faint of heart. It's the kind of thing you only to resort to in an alley in Moscow. And these guys both look like they could lift a truck. Maybe two. So, you see, I have no choice.

Katerina does not hesitate for a second. I mean, like an effing bobcat, she is in motion and the two of us are basically double-teaming these three hundred pounds of dimwitted muscle for the next two minutes. I will spare you the boring details, other than an exemplary flying kick and cobra punch my dojo master would be proud of, which sends meathead number two into the concrete. Fun fact: Katerina's meathead is already on the ground. If I ever thought *I* was good, it would seem Katerina is better.

The destructor in me salutes the destructor in her. Because if I'm a black belt she's a Death Star belt.

I bet you're curious as to what Uri is doing at this time. I know I am.

Welp, he's basically standing there a little bit like Dustin Hoffman in *Rain Man*. He's observing. In a doltish kind of way. Silent. Shoulders hunched. Head cocked to one side.

I practically expect him to recite extremely hard calculus equations before asking for Jell-O and Judge Wapner.

The good thing about these guys both being the size of Mount Everest is that they are slow as snails. I mean it. They're on, like, Alabama time.

Don't tell me you've never asked for directions in Alabama. Oh, you haven't? Okay, let me just explain. If you've ever asked for directions in Alabama . . . you would still be listening now. And now. And now. And for the next five years.

But Katerina is on lightning speed. And I am at least holding up my end.

Now, finally, at the end of this romantic dance, blond meatface one and two are down for the count. Neither of them are exactly looking at each other because I think they're both pretty embarrassed they just got their asses kicked by a girl. Two girls.

I'd say this feels satisfying but, remember, I'm a pacifist.

"You are Charlie's Angels?"

Uri smiles. Katerina is whisking him down the alley, and I am following along, looking back to make sure the meat stays on the pavement.

It's about two blocks till Katerina hails a taxi and throws us in.

"Where do you never go?"

This is for Uri.

"What?"

"Where is place that you never go?"

"Church?"

"Okay. We go to church."

20

Saint Clement's Church, if it were anywhere else on Earth, except possibly Rome, would be *the* landmark everybody in town would travel from near and far to see. But, because it's in Moscow and everybody is obsessed with Saint Basil's Cathedral on Red Square, it really doesn't get the credit it deserves. I know you know Saint Basil's—it's the red one with all those colorful bobble towers on the top everybody always puts in movies to show you are in Moscow. Like the Empire State Building for New York. Or the Eiffel Tower for Paris. Saint Basil's is the establishing shot for Moscow. Here. Now you are in Moscow. See? There's that red church with all the bobbles in Red Square!

But Saint Clement's is nothing to sneeze at. Not that you

go around sneezing at churches. What are you, a satanist?

The entire thing is red, almost an orange red. With white pillars and domes everywhere. And blue onion domes, called cupolas. The blue is for Mary. And then in the middle, a cupola of gold, for God. It all hails from the Byzantine Russian Orthodox tradition, some say influenced by Persia. Which means it has the feeling of everybody just going up to it and putting more and more stuff on it until it is not only beautiful but kind of insane. And I love it. There's something so happy about it. Happy yet elegant yet shocking.

Right now, our little squad sits on a bench across the square facing out on Saint Clement's. Uri, Katerina, and me. There's a kind of post-roller-coaster-ride rush we are all feeling. Or have you ever gone bungee jumping? Afterward, you just laugh manically and feel like you have somehow cheated death. Yeah. That's what we feel like now.

I'm the first one to talk.

"Um . . . does anybody know what just happened?"

But Katerina changes the subject.

"How you know how to fight like this, American Paige?"

I shrug and try to laugh it off.

"My mom. She was sort of paranoid and wanted me to be able to defend myself."

"Defend yourself from what, nuclear bomb?" Uri scoffs.

Katerina keeps her eyes on me, not really buying it.

"While we're playing twenty questions, what's with the gun?"

"What you mean?" Katerina asks.

"You know. The death stick you are holding in your hand."

She shrugs. "I have to defend myself."

"Seriously? Here, let me see it."

Katerina hands over her gun. It's a Glock. The kind cops use. Totally unoriginal.

"Oh, cool."

This is what I say before I walk down the steps and throw it into the storm drain.

Down, down, down—*plop*. Never to be seen again.

"What the fuck?!" Katerina cannot believe I just did that. I don't blame her—*I* can't believe I just did that.

"Guns are for macho losers who don't know how to fight. And you don't need one. Clearly."

Uri and Katerina contemplate this. But I can tell they're both a bit perplexed.

"Back in the States, ninety people are killed by guns every DAY."

Katerina shrugs. Either because she fails to understand

or cares not about the import of my most recent statement. Or, you know, she wasn't that invested in said gun. Which is interesting. Those things are expensive. Maybe someone gave it to her . . . ? If it was your own property, you would be mightily pissed.

"And, a follow-up question, if I may: when exactly were you going to tell me that you were Jackie Chan?"

Katerina gives me that same knowing smile.

"When you tell me you are, what is his name? Chuck Norris. I like to keep secrets. I find it best for surprise."

"Well, I find it best for surprise, too, but it makes me wonder. Maybe I should be asking you if *you* are a spy."

"For who? Putin?"

Katerina actually spits on the sidewalk.

"Your expectorance leads me to believe you are not a fan."

Katerina looks around her, the walls have ears.

"*Of course I am fan!*" she says a little too loudly. "Why do you think I get calendar?"

Okay, we are getting somewhere. Katerina is a superhot badass who really doesn't like Putin but also carries a gun. Check.

The church gleams in front of us, lit up against the Moscow sky. Uri gets a text.

"Ah!" He texts back.

"So does anybody want to tell me what just happened back there?"

Uri looks up. "Yes, American Paige who throws guns in gutter without asking. I tell."

Katerina takes out a bottle of vodka from her pocket, in preparation.

"Again with the vodka! Do they just issue those to you when you're born?"

Katerina smirks.

"Okay, Paige." Uri leans in, whispers, "My dad is important man. And . . . sometime important man have enemies. And sometime enemy want to be important man, too."

"Sounds totally on the up-and-up."

Uri cracks a smile. "Ha! Paige, you are not anymore in Kansas, no?"

"I was never in Kansas."

"But, you see, they have to get me, too. Not just Dad. They have to get father and son. Both. You understand? Otherwise they cannot be important."

"So, you mean to tell me that my first week in Moscow I got stuck in the middle of a failed hostile takeover of Moscow's biggest kingpin?"

"Correct."

"Can I tweet that?"

"No!" Katerina and Uri simultaneously and most emphatically declare.

"Relax. I wasn't going to." The three of us sit there, on the bench, taking in the gilded beauty of the church.

"Tell me, Uri. I'm serious. What is it like to be the son of an infamous bad guy?"

"I don't like. I want to be in America. Rap star."

Katerina and I share a look. Even she doesn't have the heart to tell him his rap artist dreams may not be coming true.

"What about you, Katerina? Is your dad a notorious kingpin, too?"

"No, my dad is dead asshole who beat us."

Whoa.

"I'm really sorry. I mean, that's horrible."

"You want to know why I have black belt? There you go. Don't worry. We do not have to talk about. We are Russian. We do not talk about feelings all the time and no one has shrink."

"I think you all have a shrink. And I think the shrink's name is vodka."

This gets a smile out of both of them.

Katerina turns to me.

"What about you, American Paige? Do your parents live

in a house in suburb with little white picket fence and fluffy dog?"

"No. My parents got kidnapped in Syria and may at this moment be dead."

This lands with a thud.

Silence.

The three of us stare straight ahead. I can feel Katerina and Uri exchange a look. I think they really did assume I was some girl from the suburbs with Bieber posters all over my wall and a few American Girl dolls in my closet for sentimental value.

Somehow saying this out loud, about my parents, makes everything worse. Maybe it is better to bury your feelings in a tsunami of booze. Before I know it, my eyes start to well up, as I look across and up toward heaven at the gold-and-blue spires with crosses on the top.

Katerina and Uri, on each side of me, put their arms around me. I sit there for a second, sandwiched between my two Moscow hosts as a tear makes it down my face. We stay this way for a while.

It's not fake. Or forced. Or claustrophobic the way I usually feel when confronted with emotion.

This is probably the most I've felt in a while. Maybe years.

I better stop.

Uri hands me the bottle and I scoff.

"Crying over vodka. Am I Russian now?"

"No. You are still lightweight," Katerina says.

Uri nudges me. "But don't worry, Paige in book. Before long, we make you heavyweight."

21

Congratulations!

You've made it to Operation Make Raynes Fall in Love With Me, Part Two: Electric Boogaloo.

For the record, I would like to admit that my stalking isn't working very well. I've been back to Café Treplev about five times, and not one of those times has Sean Raynes appeared.

If you're wondering whether Madden is getting impatient with me, the answer is yes. If you're wondering whether I sort of lost my red Beats headphones, the answer is also yes. I've lost them under my bed, on purpose.

Look, is it my fault he seems to have gone sour on Café Treplev? No. It is not.

I've actually been to about four different cafés in the general vicinity and, in every case, I've come up bust.

Today I'm trying a new café, **Главная**, pronounced "Glavnaya," which means *home* in Russian.

And it does feel like home. If, when I was at home, I was casually stalking America's number one enemy/patriot. There are mustard-colored sofas and a few plaid armchairs, table lamps. It's not a bad place. Although you never know who sits in these armchairs. And for how long. Kind of like the Starbucks armchairs back home. When you think about who might have been sitting there, and what transmittable diseases they might have, that comfy-looking cushion just starts to strongly resemble a petri dish. Or a flea factory. Or a lice hotel.

I'm on my third espresso, and I'd say my heart rate is somewhere between nervous fourth grader at a spelling bee and tooth-deprived Mississippi meth-head.

This café is a bust.

Which, actually? I am surprised. I had convinced myself that there was some outside force guiding me to this place. You know, like my feet were just kind of leading, and here it was, and somehow this was all going to manifest itself into success. Like, the Force was with me. But I guess my Jedi training is incomplete. All I've managed to manifest is a slight hungover ache compliments of Katerina's never-ending vodka march of death.

Speaking of hangovers. Everybody knows that the only real cure is a grilled cheese, french fries, and a Coke.

Don't judge me. These are desperate circumstances. I am hungover in a foreign land on a failed fact-finding mission. I need comfort food, and you and I both know we passed a diner on the way over here.

Okay. Frendy's American Diner it is!

Just setting foot in this place I feel a sense of relief. I truly hate to be this blatantly American, but I guess I am, on a kind of molecular level.

There's black-and-white checkered floors, booths, a juke-box, records hung on the ceiling. Someone has decided to play Elvis. Fine with me.

Love me tender, love me true, all my dreams fulfilled . . .

I am pretty sure Elvis was not talking about his dreams being fulfilled by french fries and a Coke, but you never know. We *are* talking about Elvis here.

I sit at one of the booths and order a grilled cheese, french fries, a Coke, a root beer float, and apple pie.

And, yes, the waiter does give me a look.

She's an older waitress in a red apron kind of thing and a white-and-red hat. The whole thing is very kitschy. I would compliment her on it, but she doesn't really seem to like me.

(No one in Russia ever seems to like you. It's how they do.)

"I'm ordering for two," I say, clutching my belly. But she doesn't get the joke. It doesn't really translate.

There are little mini jukeboxes at every table, and I catch my reflection, briefly, before looking away.

I am an impostor. A sham. It's pretty clear that I was really not the person to do this job. I mean, someone like Katerina? Definitely. But me? Weird, socially awkward, never-met-a-tangent-she-didn't-follow *me*? I honestly think Madden overestimated me. They all did.

It's okay. Root beer float, you understand me.

I disappear into an American-comfort-food vortex, where all my thoughts and worries and fears are turned into a magical smorgasbord of grease. Then I pay the bill. I am getting up to leave, feeling sorry for myself. I am pretty sure my waitress is feeling sorry for me, too.

I can practically hear her thoughts:

Poor American girl. So fat, ignorant, and alone.

I'm just about to shuffle out of there in a fit of shame when it happens.

There. Walking in and taking a seat at the bar.

There.

All alone.

Sean Raynes.

22

Ho. LEE. Crap.

I see Sean Raynes in the moment when I am halfway out the door, but, when I see him, my left leg stops and tries to turn around. But my right leg is stubbornly continuing forward. So basically half of me is leaving and half of me is turned sideways, perpendicular to myself. And I'm frozen.

If you are wondering if I look cool in this moment, the answer is a most definite no. In all honesty, I kind of look mentally deranged or like a first grader who is struck by a sudden and intense urge to pee. The waitress looks at me frozen in spazdom and raises an eyebrow.

But Sean Raynes does not—thank you, Jesus.

Instead, Sean Raynes sits at the counter, picks up a

menu, and orders french fries.

Ladies and gentlemen, America's most notorious hero/traitor is eating french fries.

See, it's not just me. You really can't be out of the States too long before you start missing what normally you would consider lame, plebeian, and ordinary. No matter how erudite you consider yourself to be.

I can see bodyguard and possible Dark Lord, Oleg, out the window keeping watch. I guess Raynes must have wanted some space.

The question is . . . what the hell do I do now?

If I leave, then there's absolutely no point to this random, fortuitous encounter, which I can only consider a gift from the gods. If I stay, when I was clearly out the door, I might look like a stalker or even blow my cover.

I know! I'll go to the ladies' room.

See, that is what is called taking lemons and making lemonade. It looks like I have to pee, so now I am using that to my advantage. I am brilliant!

I make a beeline for the bathroom before he can see me. Again, the waitress gives me a look. Wow. She is *so* not into me.

The bathroom in here is red, white, and blue. So much 'murica! I take this opportunity to make myself look vaguely presentable after my food bender.

If I let my hair down, pinch my cheeks, and put on natural-blush-shade Burt's Bees chapstick, which is all I have, I don't look entirely horrible.

And I am talking to myself.

"Think, Paige, think. C'mon. What do I say? What do I do? How do I not make it obvious?"

I have a really cool plan to saunter back in and say something extremely pithy about kitsch, which is exactly what I do in my imagination. But what happens in reality is . . . as I pass by Raynes I slip on what I can only imagine is a discarded french fry on the black-and-white checkered floor and actually *trip*.

Into Sean Raynes.

You see, I *am* supercool. It's really hard to be this suave, so don't be intimidated.

Once again, the waitress is sizing me up. Is she smirking? I get the feeling she's going to go home tonight and tell her boyfriend about me: *There was weird girl at place today. Almost like circus freak.*

You've really never lived until you've slipped on a french fry and plowed into an enemy of the state. I do it all the time. Really.

The very best thing is, Raynes was drinking a soda, and now that soda is everywhere.

He turns to me, annoyed.

"Jesus!"

"I'm so sorry. God, I'm such an idiot. I just—I tripped and I think there was, like, a french fry or something and—"

"What?"

"On the floor? I think there was a french fry? And I slipped on it."

My entire face is a squiggly mouth.

"Wait a minute." He squints at me. "You! Were you at Café Treplev the other day?"

Aha! He remembers me.

"Guilty."

I try to smile demurely. I don't think I'm pulling it off.

"You were wearing an Elliott Smith T-shirt, right?"

"Guilty again. Wow. Quite a memory you have."

"Well, you don't exactly see that many girls walking around Moscow in a 'SAY YES' shirt."

"You don't say . . ."

Now it's just a *little* bit awkward. The waitress comes over to clean everything up and, I swear to God, gives me a look like *WTF is wrong with you?*

"Well, I'm sorry. Again. For like the millionth time. If there's anything I can do . . . I'd offer to pay for your dry cleaning, but you're wearing a T-shirt, and that's just, like, weird—I mean, who dry-cleans their T-shirts? Plus, there's no, like, environmentally sound organic dry cleaners in

Moscow, I'm assuming, so I would have to, like, send it back home, have it dry-cleaned there and then sent BACK to Moscow, and that would probably take forever and it would more than likely just get lost, but it's an ethical and moral issue really . . ."

And now both the waitress and Sean Raynes are staring at me.

I hear there are new technologies involving invisibility cloaks and, I have to say, if I could put on an invisibility cloak right this second and just kind of disappear—POOF—I totally. Effing. Would.

Ladies and gentlemen, Frendy's American Diner in Moscow is completely silent. I mean, I think a tumbleweed just rolled out between the counter and the jukebox.

"Do you want to get a drink?"

Sean Raynes says it out of nowhere. Like it pops out of him. An involuntary spasm of *What the hell?*

"Um. Are you talking to me?"

I look around behind me.

The waitress rolls her eyes.

"Yeah, I am . . . talking to you."

"Oh, that was just my Robert De Niro imitation."

He cocks his head. He's kind of looking at me, honestly, the way you would look at your kid sister if she was rolling around on the floor at your birthday party. It's not hatred.

It's just a curious look of endearment.

I don't think I've blown it. Implausibly. Somehow.

Finally, the waitress just can't take it anymore.

"You know this girl is weirdo, yes?"

"Yes." He nods. "I know this girl is weirdo. C'mon, weirdo, let's go."

23

Have you ever been on a romantic stroll involving you, an internationally famous expat, and a swarthy bodyguard? I have to tell you, it's a bit awkward. Raynes and I walk out into the brisk, autumn air and down the path next to the Moskva River. All very intimate. Except the surly bodyguard part.

The three of us (or likely more but whoever else is with us is in disguise) duck down an alley somewhere behind the Bolshoi Theatre, and Raynes walks familiarly up to a dark brown door with no distinguishing qualities.

He knocks. Oleg stands there looking impatient.

A teeny-tiny rectangular slit opens up and a set of eyeballs looks through.

"пароль?" the mysterious eyes ask. (*Password?*)

"беспредел," Raynes replies. (*Bespredel.*)

(Translation: *lawlessness.*)

The sluggish brown door opens, and Raynes and I, escorted by our dearest Oleg, wind down a long hall, taking two rights and then a left, into a hallway with a black door. There's an enormous man in a gray turtleneck and black pants standing stoically in front of this door. He nods imperceptibly at Raynes before opening the door.

Walking into this place is a bit like walking into a 1940s film noir set in a Bangkok opium den. As soon as you step through the curtains, under the dim light of the red lanterns, everything becomes a smoldering shade of red.

The scarlet hues and ornate circular room dividers give way from a central bar area to a fairly low-key and empty back area. I'm guessing this is where Raynes likes to hide from the adoring/hateful throngs.

We sit next to one of the circular room dividers, creating a little nook where no one can really see us. Oleg takes a seat at the bar. Thank God.

I really did not want to have to make conversation with Oleg.

(*So . . . strangle anyone today?*)

A stick-thin waitress with red lipstick in a deep crimson silk Hong Kong dress approaches. Her hair is in a bun with those little sticks in it.

I'm too busy being nervous to notice she's been standing there awhile.

"Do you know what you want? The big hit here is the mai tais."

"Oh, um, okay, I'll have a mai tai."

He orders a whiskey. Mmmm-kay?

"So, um . . . did you come to Moscow just to spill drinks on strangers?"

"Yes. I can't wait to spill my mai tai on you."

He smirks. His expression is so warm, and now, so are my cheeks. Something strange is happening here. I don't want to say it's, like, Hallmark-card rainbow time. That's not it. It's like both of us are trying to talk to each other without really looking at each other. Like without making eye contact.

Like we're both thinking what I am thinking, which is, Oh my God, are you actually real? Like a flesh-and-blood person?

And then . . . we do make eye contact and it's like an electric shock. *Zap.* And we both look away.

And neither of us knows exactly what to do with this. Or, at least, I don't.

I remember this French expression: *coup de foudre.* Lightning bolt. A kind of love at first sight. I remember thinking it was ridiculous. I mean, how can you just meet someone and instantly feel like you can't look at them because whatever is happening between you is too powerful? That is a fairy tale—like a unicorn or a leprechaun with a pot of gold at the end of a rainbow.

Except it sure feels like exactly what is happening right now.

"So, you're a student?"

"Um . . . yes."

There's an awkward silence.

He doesn't know if I know who he is or not. If I'm aware that he's *the* Sean Raynes. I can tell he kind of wants to ask but doesn't know how to without seeming like a pompous jerk.

"Look, I'm just gonna be honest with you. I think it would be sort of disingenuous of me to pretend I don't actually know that you are, um . . . who you are."

I leave out the part about being an international spy. Also, the part about my feels. I exclude the fact that my heart seems to be skipping.

He sighs. I think it's a sigh of relief.

"Well, at least now I don't have to explain the bodyguards. Or bodyguard. Who knows? I can never really tell how many there are. Which is weird."

We both look at Oleg. Really, we can just see the back

of him, but even his shoulders are mean, slanted forward, ready to strike.

"Does he follow you into the shower?"

"Yes, it's actually kind of helpful. Especially the part where he scrubs my back. You can never really thoroughly exfoliate there yourself."

We both laugh a little, but it's an uncomfortable laugh.

Our drinks come, and we both sit there a second, slurping in silence.

I decide to break the ice.

"Um. Do you mind if I ask you something?"

"Shoot."

"What does it feel like to be here? And to be you. Here?"

He looks at me, weighing his answer.

"Hmm . . . Do you want the cool answer or the honest answer?"

"Maybe both?"

"Okay, well the cool answer is . . . It's amazing, it's fantastic. I did it! I showed them all!"

"And the honest answer . . . ?"

"Can you keep a secret?"

"Um. Yes." I think I'm keeping a really big one right now.

"You're not a journalist or anything?"

"Nope. Definitely not."

"It's kind of lonely. And I'm homesick."

He takes a drink and I sip my mai tai.

Oleg turns to stare at us. He's not even pretending to be casual.

"Is that why you were eating french fries at Frendy's American Diner?"

"That's exactly why I was eating french fries at Frendy's American Diner. And you?"

"Do you want the cool answer or the honest answer?"

"Both."

"The cool answer is . . . well, there is no cool answer. The honest answer is I'm homesick, too. Which makes me feel like a dumb American. I really thought I was more sophisticated than I actually am."

There's a moment of nothing here, and then this comes out . . .

"It's nice to talk to someone from back home."

Uh, we both said that. At the same time. In the same way.

"Okay, that was weird."

"Yes, it was. Obviously, you are a robot."

"No, human. I am not," I say in my best robot voice. God, I'm a nerd.

He smiles.

"Okay, I have a follow-up question. If everyone always comes up to you everywhere you go and wants to be nice to you, because you're famous, maybe that's not so lonely . . . ?"

"Yeah, but . . . does that really sound like fun to you? Hey, will you come out with me while I stare at you the whole time?!"

"Okay, you're right. Just so you know, that's kind of what it feels like to be a girl walking in front of a construction site. In case you were curious."

"Ah. I see. I never thought about it before."

There's something about him that stays right here, right here in this moment. He's not checking his phone or trying to think of the next thing. It's like he's just taking it in. Letting the wheels go round and round.

Oleg turns from the bar and nods to him. These Russians sure don't smile much.

"I guess I have to get going. They're really paranoid about me. Like I'm sort of their prize pony. They don't want to lose me."

"I bet you wish the US had revoked your passport over somewhere else. Like Zermatt? Or Edinburgh?"

"I know." Then he frowns. "Wait. How did you know they revoked my passport? Most people just think I defected, because I'm a godless traitor commie spy."

Oops. I know because my top secret government agency handler told me.

Deflect, dummy! Deflect!

"I'm not most people. And, um, I think you're a hero."

God, I hope I didn't blow it by saying that. Ugh. Why did I just say that?

"Um . . . Do you want to have dinner sometime?"

"Me?"

"You're the only other person in the room. Besides Oleg. And I have dinner with him every night. So I've kind of lost that loving feeling."

"Did you just quote Hall & Oates?"

"Ironically."

"There is no other way to quote Hall & Oates."

"I can quote many other things ironically at dinner."

I giggle.

Giggling. So not cool.

"There's this restaurant I really like. Ramallah Café. Do you like meze?"

"Oh, I love it. My dad is a really big fan."

I don't know why I said that.

"Well, I think you might kind of like this place. It's all sandstone and gardens. It's like being in the Middle East. Without the explosions."

"And the never-ending tension and hopelessness?"

"Exactly. Maybe you could meet me there . . . tomorrow? Is that too soon? Is that desperate? I'm not really very good at this."

"Yes! No! I will meet you there." God, I'm like stuck in staccato or something. I sound like an engine backfiring.

"Okay. Good. Maybe meet me there at eight?"

"Ramallah Café. Eight o'clock."

Oleg rolls his eyes and grabs Raynes out of this extremely nervous interaction. Thank God.

Raynes is whisked away by Swarthy McSwarthington and now it's just me. Just me and my mai tai.

There's a lot of colorful things happening right now. This place is ruby red. The umbrella in my drink is sunset orange. And the butterflies in my stomach are . . . I don't know. Butterfly colored. Blue. Maybe orange and black. Maybe monarchs. Whatever color they are, they are bustling. They are fluttering around and making me feel like they might just fly me up into the air with them.

I want to say his name. I want to shout it into the air: *Sean Raynes! I am going on a date with Sean Raynes!* And then I want to say his name quietly to myself, keep it secret. A whisper.

What is happening to me? None of this is familiar.

I don't have crushes. I have booty calls.

So this *realizing* of crushes is kind of a new thing.

And also, I have to say, I can't tell if I am excited more by having dinner tomorrow night with America's public enemy number one in a West Bank–inspired restaurant, or telling

Madden I am having dinner tomorrow night with America's public enemy number one in a West Bank–inspired restaurant.

Mother would be so proud.

24

Two flights up the steps to my dorm, I see Uri. He's practicing some actually not horrible pop-and-lock moves, listening to his headphones. I wave my hand in front of him to wake him from his hip-hop slumber.

"American Paige! Just the girl I see!"

"Yes, Uri, to what do I owe the pleasure of this impromptu dorm break dancing? By the way, you should break-dance outside, where there is less lead to inhale."

"Lead? Is bad?"

"Yes, is very bad. And it's probably in every building on campus. So stay outside often. Speaking of which, let's take this out on the green, shall we?"

Uri frowns. "Are all Americans paranoid?"

"Just because you're paranoid doesn't mean they're not after you."

"Ah! I like this! Just because paranoid doesn't mean they are after you."

"Okay, that's not—"

"Great!"

So, now Uri and I are barreling out the front steps and on to the main green of the quad. A few students give him a passing look, as I'm sure he's achieved a level of John-Gotti's-son fame on campus.

"So, Uri, spit it out. What do you need? Are you here to pledge your undying love for Katerina?"

"No. I am here for help."

"For help who?"

"For help you. My American BFF . . . F."

"And what, possibly, do you think would be necessary in this regard?"

Uri leans in, whispers, "Paige, remember how you said parents were gone, taken in horrible place and disappear?"

Oh God. I don't even know if I want to hear this next sentence.

"Paige, I can help. You see . . ." And now this is an even softer whisper. "My father, he get things, from strange places. Places you are not supposed to get from."

This freezes my breath inside my body.

"It is possible, he even get little information from man who gets it from man who gets it from somebody else. Someone who has seen parents. Someone who could maybe get parents out. For price."

The number of thought bubbles swirling around my head, I would put at around three hundred.

"USA, Paige, they don't pay price. They hate negotiate. But my father. He is used to negotiate. He is expert."

Okay, so basically what's happening is Uri is offering me the chance to find my parents and pay a ransom to bring them home. Good plan. Except I would get the ransom from . . . who?

"Uri, I don't have that kind of money."

"I do. My dad does." He puffs up his chest and smiles. "*I pay.*"

"Uri, I can't do that. As much as I wish I could. And, believe me, I reeeeeeeally wish I could. I just couldn't take that kind of money. Nothing good would come of it. I just know it."

"Are you sure? Maybe would not be that much?"

"Uri, have you ever heard the expression, 'If you lie down with dogs, you get up with fleas'?"

Uri pouts. "Am I flea?"

"NO! No, you are not flea, Uri. You are great. You are wonderful and I like you a lot—"

"Like for sex?"

"No, not like for sex. But like for friendship. Closeness. Caring."

What am I talking about. Caring? I've never said the word *caring* in my life. But I do like Uri. I do feel a sense of closeness, and I think it's called . . . *kindness* with him. Like a human feeling. And the fact that he's even thinking about my parents, that it's been on his mind, that means something. He didn't just shrug it off and throw it away that night at the church. He thought about it. He wanted to fix it.

"But the thing is . . . I'm pretty sure my parents wouldn't really want me to get involved . . . in this manner . . . with certain . . . elements."

"Like fleas."

"Uri, it really means a lot to me that you would try. It does. But I just can't."

"Okay, fine, be that way."

"Uri, your English is getting a lot better."

"Maybe good, but I don't understand your culture. Why everybody smile all the time? Petrodollars?"

"Could be, Uri. Could be that we're all sort of at Disneyland while the world is burning all around us."

"That was dark for American. Maybe you are turning Russian."

The sky behind him slices over the campus in sheets of

gray, a canopy of wisps, spreading out over the horizon.

I'm not sure if I want to ask this, but it blurts itself out.

"Uri?"

"Yes, dark American."

"Do you think it would be possible to maybe ask around, though? Like ask someone if they had maybe heard something from a guy who maybe had heard something from another guy, kind of thing? About—just—whether they're alive?"

"Just question?"

"Yes. Just question. That's all. Just like you're curious."

"Like *Oh, I am so curious about random American couple who I have nothing to do with?*"

"Yeah."

"Okay, Paige. For you, I do this."

"Uri . . . why for me you do this?"

He looks at me a second, tilts his head. Then laughs.

"Ah! You have paranoid thought! See! You *are* turning Russian!"

I can't help but smile.

"Relax, uptight person. It called friendship. Look it in dictionary."

"Ah. Friendship."

"Yes. It is clear I am your first friend. That is okay. I teach you the ways."

And with that Uri lunges in, gives me a kiss on the cheek, and exits dramatically across the quad.

"Hey, Uri!"

He turns.

"Thanks."

He does a kind of tip of the hat and continues his peacock walk away over the green. An undiscovered supermodel walks past him and he grabs his heart, looking at her as if he's been shot.

25

My favorite thing about the spy-girl gig is this part. The science of steganography. Sending Madden correspondence by embedding messages within other, seemingly benign sites. So far, it's definitely the most James Bond part of the job. Hands down.

I update him on my romantic interlude with Raynes and of our next rendezvous at Ramallah Café. Despite himself, he seems impressed.

Here at the bird-watchers website, I upload a picture of a waxwing on a white beam tree with my message securely encrypted in the bird's talons. It's actually a pretty simple process of altering the last two bits of each byte in the image, which changes the photo imperceptibly, but allows you to free up the necessary space to hide a message in the pixels.

Okay, now you try it.

Katerina is at class, and I have no intention of telling *her* about Raynes. Because, let's be honest. Something is wrong here.

I don't really *believe* she's FSB, because that seems kind of paranoid and delusional, but . . .

I've been weighing it and it seems too wonky to be random.

The fact that she had a gun, the fact that she didn't really seem to care when I threw said gun out, the fact that she's a black belt and then some . . . none of that really makes sense. If it was her *actual* gun, wouldn't she have been pissed to lose it?

The only way you wouldn't freak out in that situation is if the gun *wasn't yours*. Like, say, if maybe you worked for an intelligence agency.

I don't think it's a stretch to wonder if maybe she's FSB.

I asked Madden to look into it. In the meantime, though, the question is . . . If she actually is, after all, an FSB spy, then was she put in my room as my roommate because that's just par for the course with American foreign exchange students? Or was she put there specifically for me?

Because if she was put there specifically for me, that means my cover's blown.

And if my cover's blown, that means I have to leave.

Which means no meze at Ramallah Café.

And no more flirtation with Raynes.

Which would be tragic.

But *also* it would mean my shot at bringing my parents home was lost.

And that loss is unacceptable.

26

Just so you know, it's not stalking if you are on an assignment.

Yes, some people would consider it weird to Google someone for over two hours and to go down each and every possible rabbit hole heretofore known to man just to catch a glimpse, a glimmer, a spark, of the character of said person inside said rabbit hole.

A clue. A tidbit. A pithy moment of revelation.

All of these clicks, every one, trying to reach further and further into the mind, soul, heart, veins, body of the most notable expat in recent history.

Here, in the middle of the night, with Katerina out probably getting pie-eyed on vodka once again, I am free, alone, able to throw it all to hell and find out everything, every odd fact there is to know about my obsession. I mean, my assignment.

And just like with any assignment, it pays to do your research.

I've spent an hour just on Google image search, looking into his eyes online and wondering if they're the eyes of a monster or of the kind of person who can fall in love.

27

And we're back! To the mysterious video footage! Come with me, won't you, on this magical tour? Remember, I don't know any of this is happening at this time. I don't see it until later. Praise the sweet, sweet Lord.

So—the Baroque dining room with the gilded everything and sky-blue ceiling? Well, here we are again. For lunch.

Dimitri, Queen Elsa, and Underling are seated in white Louis Catorce dining chairs.

"Who are these stupid girls?"

It's Ice Queen. She's pointing at a photograph, taken off a still from a security camera.

And guess who the two stupid girls are? Yup. You guessed

it. Katerina and me. And between us there is Uri. International rap nonphenomenon. I'm guessing this came from the night of the bang-bang shoot-out in the cool bunker bar.

Bald kingpin Dimitri seems unconcerned.

"Who? Them? Who knows. You know my son. He has revolving door."

Queen Elsa blows out smoke in disgust. Takes a shot of vodka. And then another one.

Next to them is Underling, offering picture after picture for Dimitri's perusal. "The bidders you wanted me to cultivate," he explains.

Dimitri flip, flip, flips.

"What about him? This guy?"

They are both looking down at a photograph of an extremely conservative-looking man. A website screen grab from his "foundation." A banner at the top of the image says, "Restoring American Values."

"He is white racist. Calls himself patriot. Billionaire. He could bid high. Maybe highest."

Flip.

"And him?" Now they are staring at a picture of an Asian man in a green khaki shirt with epaulets.

"He is small-time North Korean establishment. Wants to be big-time. He made offer. Low offer."

"How low?" Dimitri tilts his head, squinting at the shot of the low bidder.

"One million."

Dimitri scoffs. Rips the picture in two.

"There are a few more. One in Venezuela. But who knows? Unstable. Also, a drug kingpin in Jalisco. Probably will be dead soon."

"How much did he offer?"

"Two million."

Dimitri scoffs again.

"These are lowball. Keep looking."

Queen Elsa snorts.

"What is problem, *mishka?*"

She shrugs.

"And what about Raynes? Is Oleg still guarding his nest like baby bird?"

"They all are. But look at this. He has girlfriend."

Underling sets a picture down of Sean Raynes with none other than . . . yours truly. Paige Nolan! Internationally renowned superspy! Someone's *girlfriend!*

This must have been taken when we were walking down the Moskva River to the Hong Kong bar. Oleg follows behind, looking suspicious and generally surly.

"Ah."

"She is Russian?"

"Not sure. Raynes doesn't speak Russian, so—"

"Maybe he speak international language," Queen Elsa snarks.

Dimitri looks at her, annoyed.

But then something catches his eye. Something on the table in front of Ice Queen. The black-and-white picture from the bunker bar.

"Wait."

He picks up the picture. Now he picks up the picture from the Moskva River.

"I don't believe."

Underling and Queen Elsa wait.

"Look at that girl."

Underling and Queen Elsa take in the black-and-white photograph. The one from the bunker bar shoot-out with Uri.

"Now look at that girl. Here."

Underling and Queen Elsa look at the Moskva River photograph. The one with Sean Raynes and me, strolling along by the water.

"Do you see?"

Silence.

"It is same girl!"

And now it dawns on the both of them. It *is* same girl.
And that same girl happens to be me. Ladies and gentlemen,
Paige Nolan, at your service.

Dimitri looks at Underling.

"You. Get me that girl."

28

It's sunrise, which means check-in/exercise time with Madden. Currently, I am being yelled at as I run past Red Square and Saint Basil's Cathedral, bobbling into the morning light.

"You're moving too slowly, Paige. This isn't *Romeo and Juliet*."

"Fucker, I have to make him trust me, and to make him trust me takes time."

Two babushkas give me a disapproving look outside the cathedral.

"You know, you're not the only one interested in Sean Raynes, Paige."

"I know. You are. RAITH is. I get it."

"No, what I mean is, we're not the only ones."

"I know. FSB. Putin. Embarrassment. America bashing. Got it."

"There's more."

"Really? Who?"

"The mob."

"Are you serious?"

"As a heart attack. Our sources say that the Russian mafia is planning to kidnap Raynes and sell him to the highest bidder. Could be Boko Haram, could be the Islamic State, could be Piers fucking Morgan for all we know. The point is, if you think this guy's a hero? Whatever he has, wherever he has it, we need you to figure it out what it is. Like yesterday."

"So, the clock is ticking. Time is of the essence. A stitch in time saves—"

"Paige. This isn't a joke. Do you want Raynes to die? That is, *after* all his state secrets are tortured out of him by God knows who?! By Iran? By North Korea? By fucking ISIS? Is that what you want?"

I stop, panting, on the bridge over the Moskva River, stunned by the Cathedral of Christ the Saviour. It stands unimpressed, white and gold spires gleaming in the sunrise, lording over the bridge like the Taj Mahal. You would never believe this place could be so beautiful.

"Maybe state secrets shouldn't be such secrets."

"No. Trust me, Paige. You don't want that."

"Who watches the watchers, Madden? How do you—"

"Jesus Christ, I have a level-one security clearance and I *know*. Okay? So why don't you do your job?"

He hangs up.

In front of me, the gold baubles on the top of the cathedral reach up to the sky, one giant gold bauble in the middle, making its way up to heaven.

Why *don't* I do my job?

The church stares back at me, waiting for an answer.

29

You know that feeling? That feeling you get when it seems like you and he are the only two people in the world? Like every moment before this was leading to this instant—this one here, when it's just you two. Against the world?

No? Let me explain.

We are in the middle of a sandstone, tree-lined garden on a rooftop in Moscow. I have no idea how they managed to make it seem, in the middle of this vast and cold-getting-colder city, like we are somewhere just footsteps from Damascus Gate in the Old City of Jerusalem. It's truly an ambitious project. I'll tell you one thing: whoever built this was homesick. That or, considering all the exotically themed locales I've inhabited during this excursion, Russia has kidnapped a trove of Disney Imagineers to use at their whim.

There must be some kind of enclosure all around the edge of this roof, because inside, in the row of wooden mother-of-pearl-inlaid tables and chairs, with what looks like some kind of hanging garden above us, it's cozy and warm, whereas outside it's dipping down to whatever that is when you start to see your breath.

Across from me, framed by the grape leaves dripping from the pergola above, is the singular presence that is Sean Raynes.

There are hanging metal lanterns with mosaic colors glittering everywhere, adding to the feeling that we just might be eating in the Garden of Eden. Before the fall.

Raynes's eyes are deep set and intense. I don't know if this is just me, or if they would be that way for anyone. But I almost can't stand looking at him. It's too much. Like I feel it's just going to throw me across the room.

Oleg sits a few tables away, in all his surly glory, as I try to guess Sean's favorite novel.

"*The Catcher in the Rye.*"

He laughs. "Nope. Too obvious."

"Okay, give me a hint."

The waiter comes over bringing the meze: hummus, olives, tahini, tabouleh, and everything else delicious from the dawn of civilization.

"Okay. A hint. Hmm. It's set in World War Two."

"Is it . . . *The Painted Bird*?"

"Wait. What? How did you guess that?! Seriously? How the hell did you just guess that?"

I smile. "Elementary, my dear Raynes. That's a book about somebody who is an outsider. I think maybe you see yourself as an outsider. Also, it's a great book."

"Okay, but I mean, *The Sun Also Rises*, *Catch-22*, *Maus*? You could have picked any of those. Why—"

"You're not the only one who feels like a painted bird."

This sits there for a second.

I wasn't trying to have a heartfelt moment, honestly. It really just slipped out. Now I feel vulnerable. And scared. And maybe like my heart just stopped.

"Well. I also have a runner-up favorite book, but it's non-fiction. About the Navajo rebellion on Fortress Rock. It's a pretty amazing story. Nobody really knows about it. The history's been buried."

"Ooo. Do tell."

"Basically when all the Navajos where being marched off their land, you know, the Long Walk, this group of them held a meeting and crafted a plan to rebel. So they went up this impossibly tall rock, called Fortress Rock, which is seven hundred practically vertical feet, using only wooden ladders. And then they brought the ladders up. So the army couldn't get up there. They had to just sit there at the bottom and wait for them. And it wasn't just men. It was women and children. Pregnant women going up this insanely steep rock, almost like a skyscraper, on these wooden ladders."

"Really? Wait. Did it work?"

"Yeah, it did. The army was really cocky at first. They thought the Navajos would have to come down. For food, for water. But guess what?"

"I'm on the edge of my seat."

"After about a month, they *were* running out of water. So they waited until the army was asleep, and they formed basically this human chain down the rock. They sent one guy to go fetch the water. Then he came back, and they brought all the water back up the rock through the human chain of hands, just one by one, all the way up the rock."

"Wow. That's pretty cool."

"And guess what happened then? The *army* ran out of food. And they had to leave. They gave up."

"Seriously?"

"Yes. And there are still Navajo people to this day who come from that family line. It's kind of like a badge of pride. *The ones who never surrendered.*"

"I love that story. I love everything about that story."

He smiles but then notices something beyond me.

"Oh my God."

"What?" I duck like there's an assassin over my shoulder. Which, you know, *possible*.

"Look, come sit over here for a second. Don't look up. Not until I say."

"Okay, I shall keep my eyes averted."

I sit next to Raynes and shield my eyes.

"Now. Ready? Open them."

I open my eyes to see the most enormous, orange full moon coming over the horizon, just above the city lights. It looks like you could just reach up and climb right up on top of it and ride it off into the cosmos.

"Wait. Wait. I have the perfect thing."

And now Raynes is rummaging through his coat, and next thing I know, we both have earphones on and Elliott Smith is playing on his iPhone.

I'll tell you why I
don't want to know where you are . . .
I got a joke
I've been dying to tell you . . .

We lean back, listening to the most wistful, melodic, sad voice and looking at the giant tangerine moon, and we are in it together, just the two of us. And there's no one else in the world. Anywhere.

Except the waiter.

He comes over in all his waiter hustle and bustle but stops short when he sees us, and decides to leave us alone.

And he *should* leave us alone.

Everyone should leave us alone.

Because it's just him and me.

And it is

everything.

30

The good news is that on my light morning jog I see Uri.

It's seven in the morning, I am the picture of health, mind/body spirit connection, and yoga-style living, and there he drives up . . . in a bright yellow Humvee, blasting DMX. You know, just fitting in.

He calls out from the driver's side.

"Aha! I caught you! American bouncing girl!"

"I think you mean running . . . ?"

"Tell me, what are you running away from, little health rat?!"

"Wait, did you mean to say *nut*? Like *health nut*?"

"Come, I have emergency."

"I'd like to, but I think I might be allergic to brightly colored Humvees, so . . ."

"You funny! Funny, bouncing girl! Get in car."

"Okay, but I'm really just getting in so you stop saying that. Also, for the record, this is not a low-energy-emission vehicle."

Uri imitates me: "Also, for record, you kill doves with your happiness . . ."

"Okay, fine. I'm getting in. Also, that was not a very flattering imitation, by the way."

I hop over to shotgun, where it's basically a twenty-foot step up to get in.

"This is obviously not made for little people."

"No, it is made for big, strong Russian with huge testicle!" He flexes his muscle, gesticulating over the music.

"I'm not sure that's how you want to phrase—"

"Now we go to emergency."

"Okay, what's the emergency?"

He turns to me, dead serious.

"Gucci."

Seriously? Facepalm.

31

Ladies and gentlemen of the jury, I did not have any intention of entering this store. This kind of place, to be true,
just gives me the heebie-jeebies. You know, this place with
three giant gold chandeliers hanging down over pristinely
displayed zillion-dollar suits.

Five giant letters outside spell the satanic words in gold:
GUCCI.

"Uri, I'm not sure I can exist in this store. I think I might
break out in hives."

But Uri is too busy looking at himself in a pair of jeans
with an embroidered black-and-white snake going up the
side, which probably cost a year of tuition.

"Relax, little mouse. You can escape in moment. I just need opinion."

"Okay, my opinion is all this conspicuous consumption is terrifying. You could feed a village with those jeans!"

"You are so funny. You are little complainer everywhere."

Maybe I am complainer everywhere, but I can't help but feel like the gleeful embrace of giddy materialism, after chucking out the Soviets, has released a kind of feverish capitalism that would make Midas blush. It's like a toddler having just eaten his first piece of candy. Money! Spending! Happiness! I just feel like telling the whole place to slow down already. It's not that great. Really, it's not at all what it's supposed to be. Easy there, new consumers. Take it slow.

But Russians don't really take things slow. And they don't really do things tentatively. Just as the giant Peter the Great statue on the Moskva River is the tallest statue in the world, weighs one thousand tons, and dwarfs everything around it, there seems to be a prevailing concept that bigger is better, more is more. I guess this is what happens when your country isn't founded by Puritans. There's a kind of lack of guilt to all of it. But maybe that's nothing new. Ask the czars.

One of the exquisitely dressed attendants comes by, holding up two suits for Uri. One gray, one navy.

"What you think?"

"I think they're perfect if you're planning on stroking a cat in your evil mountain lair."

He shakes his head no, and there goes the attendant, annoyed at me.

But before I can grumble further, Uri is next to me on the gold marble bench probably put here for bored husbands, boyfriends, or sugar daddies.

And now he's changed his tone completely, whispering, "This is safe place to talk. I want to bring you here to tell you . . . there is good news."

Wait. Is he actually talking about my parents? Here? In the middle of this golden calf? This makes no sense.

"It's not bugged," he whispers, looking around.

Ah, I get it.

But the idea of hearing anything about my parents . . . Suddenly the room slows to a stop. I brace myself.

"It's good news." He nods. "Nobody has heard anything."

"What?!" I burst out, a little too loudly. "How is that *good* news? What are you—"

"Trust me, Paige. No news is good news for the kind of people I ask. It mean they are keeping secret, for someone else, who is keeping secret for someone else. If secret is being kept . . . that means they are alive."

I'm trying to make my way around this labyrinthian logic and, somehow, halfway across the world, in the midst of this capitalist citadel, it does sort of make sense.

"There is nothing to keep secret if they are dead, no?"

He looks me in the eye, drops everything.

"But who are you—?"

He stops me there. "You don't want to know. You cannot know. These are bad people. Who know bad people. Who know other bad people. This is black market. Not world for little mouse girl."

Somehow the thought of Uri asking someone, who asks someone who asks someone else, across borders and to the darkest corners on Earth, where secrets are being kept or not kept, where lives hang in the balance, where my parents lives hang in the balance, my fucking sweet, kind, loving parents, somewhere in the darkness surrounded by vipers, is too much.

Right there in the middle of the store, amid all the decadence and promise of happiness spun in gold . . . I. Break. The. Fuck. Down.

And I can't breathe. I can't breathe in this place. No words or gestures make it possible for my lungs to gasp this air or maybe it's too much air or maybe it's not enough or maybe I am falling apart right here. My face is a wall of tears and Uri is next to me now. Sheltering.

"No, no, no. It's okay. This is good news. Paige. You are okay. I am here. Look. Okay?"

And now there are three attendants all around, con-cerned, and Uri is protecting me from them, too.

"*Vse norlmal'se. Vse norlmal'se.*"

The attendants are looking at one another, gauging, try-ing to figure out if they should call an ambulance.

Uri tells them to give us space. They retreat without a word.

I guess he comes here a lot.

I nod, a tiny little nod. The gold-and-black marble beneath us is slipping away, crumbling, and somewhere on the other side of it is everything I love and everything I am missing.

Uri holds me up, trying to make it better.

32

I'm happy to say I have completely calmed down by the time we make it back to the dorm room and the whole thing never happened. Okay, fine, it did happen and Uri is behaving in an extremely watchful, shielding manner now, which is awkward, but I am back to normal. Or whatever my version of normal is supposed to look like.

Katerina, ever blasé, turns to me and blows a smoke ring.

"I hear you freak out in store."

"Wait? How?"

"Uri call. He is protective big brother now."

Uri looks sheepish, nods, not used to this kind of role.

"It's okay, Uri. You can go. You did really well. Your dad would be proud of you."

"My dad will never be proud of me."

Okay, that sort of came out of nowhere, but maybe all my bawling and hyperventilating brought us to this come-to-Jesus moment.

"No, Uri. That's not true. I'm sure your dad—"

"Men are jealous of son. He want to be young like you." This is Katerina's pep talk. "That is why son in Greek myth kill father."

"Okay. That is enough of Katerina's Quilt of Compassion."

Uri smiles at me. "What is quilt?"

"It's, like, this thing where everybody sews together all their old scraps of clothing in squares or triangles or some kind of pattern and then sells it on Etsy for a zillion dollars. It's an American tradition. Like apple pie. Or fireworks."

"Fireworks are Chinese."

"We have a very diverse population."

Katerina puts out her cigarette, immediately lights another one.

"Okay, did you know that smoking is bad for you?"

"Did you know that running twice a day is bad for you?"

"Wait. No, it's not. And, fun fact, those things *will* kill you."

She blows her smoke at me.

"And yet we all die."

Uri looks at the two of us, a kind of friendly détente.

"You guys should make show together. Go to different village. Make joke."

"What would you call our show, Uri?"

"I would call it Sweet Naïve Live with Grim Reaper."

"Well, it has a ring to it."

Katerina smiles at me, knowingly. I can tell she really wants to ask about my new boy crush, and I desperately want to girl out and tell her everything. But none of those things are possible here.

All that's possible here is grinning and lighthearted, witty banter while inhaling secondhand smoke in a chemically dubious dorm room.

But there's nothing wrong with that, I'm learning.

In here, the three of us are like fugitives.

Hiding from forces that have coiled and wended their way into our lives—but in the end, have nothing to do with us.

33

Yeah, she's FSB."

I'm halfway past Gorky Park when Madden tells me. Jogging in my red Beats, as is my wont.

"You were right, Paige. Gold star."

"So what does that mean? Is my cover blown?"

"No. Definitely not."

"What, so it's just, like, par for the course? Every American foreign exchange student gets her own personal shadow?"

"Pretty much. I mean, maybe not every single one. She probably has multiple assignments. In the dorm. I wouldn't be surprised if your room is bugged, by the way. And videotaped."

"Ew. Really?"

"Yeah, so keep your pants on. You don't want to end up a viral sensation, now, do you?"

"Ha-ha. Very funny. Well, so what should I do?"

"Act normal."

"What about Raynes?"

"I was just about to ask you the same question."

"I'm, uh, building trust."

"Are you sure that's what you're doing? Because over here it looks like you're trying to get engaged."

"Gross! You and I both know I don't have *feelings*."

"Good. Then hurry it up. My bosses are already talking about pulling the plug on this operation."

"What?! Are you serious?"

"This isn't kindergarten, Paige."

"But—"

"*All the things* are at stake." He pauses, and I see that grainy satellite picture of my parents. "Don't make me fire you."

He hangs up.

34

I don't hear the sound as in any way related to me. It's
something in the background. Something for someone else.
White noise.

I'm halfway back to the dorm, just about to turn off the
path from Gorky Park to the river. The sun is starting to
set, not just in the sky but in the water as well, dusty hues
of pink, rose, peach, and the lights coming up one by one
in Moscow. First this streetlamp, then that one, then that
restaurant, then that light up above.

But the sound keeps coming. If anything, it's amplified.
Nearer and nearer it gets until I realize . . . Wait. That sound
is for me.

"Haaaalloooo, PAIGE . . . PAIge . . . Paige . . . paige . . ."

It's mimicking an echo. My name, from somewhere off the path.

As I turn toward the noise, it all comes crashing in, the realization of what it is, how it is, and who it is.

Below, floating right next to me down the Moskva River . . . oh God, how long has it been there? There standing on the deck of a smallish white boat . . . it's him.

Sean Raynes. In all his ebony-haired, self-deprecating, kind-of-goofy, kind-of-genius glory.

He smiles and somehow seems to lighten when I see him. Like he grows an inch taller and he exhales, somehow relieved.

"I thought you'd never see me. I've been standing out here yelling at you like an idiot for about a century."

"Oh my God. What is happening right now?"

The boat veers toward the side of the river, a limestone wall separating the river from the chaos of the city. Up ahead is a staircase down to the side of the river. I've seen fishermen down here at dawn before, first up to reel in a catch.

"What's happening is you are walking down those steps and getting in this thing. Before I get arrested for something."

"Harassment! You should be arrested for harassment!"

"Really? Is it too much?"

I want to yell out, *NO! I feel adored and magical and like I'm in a movie!* but that's not what I yell out.

"Possibly!" I say instead.

And now I'm making my way down the stone steps to the landing of the glistening but polluted Moskva River. I'm not going to lie to you, whatever those fishermen are catching here in the mornings . . . I wouldn't eat it.

And now the boat is next to the landing and I am face-to-face—well, about a foot shorter, but close enough—with Sean Raynes, international man of intrigue.

"Where's Oleg?"

I realize that the boat is being captained or driven or piloted or whatever you call it by an old salty dog who is definitely not Oleg. This guy has ivory white hair and a thousand wrinkles.

"That's what I was wondering. They sent this guy today. Maybe Oleg is getting tired of me." He dramatically raises his hands to his head. "Oh no! He's lost interest! And I just bought a new dress!"

And that is definitely a twinkle in his eye.

"Don't worry. Maybe you and this new guy will work out."

We both turn to the new guy and laugh to ourselves. He's pretty grizzled. Looks like he's seen better days.

I try to hop onto the boat but a wave comes and suddenly it actually seems like I'm going to fall between the limestone steps and the boat, directly into the ice-cold Moskva River.

"Whup!" He reaches out and grabs me, right before I am about to topple into the water, wherein the boat will probably then crush me against the sidewall and all of my trials and tribulations will be over.

The momentum pushes us both back onto the boat, where we careen backward and fall flat onto the deck.

"Jesus!"

There's a moment. Then Raynes starts laughing. I don't blame him because it's completely ridiculous.

"We are idiots," I say.

"No, we're not. We are hearty sailors."

"Yargh! And avast!"

"Is that your imitation of a hearty sailor?" He smiles down at me. We're both sitting there on the deck, recovering from our vaudeville moment. But he's right next to me, leaning over me. Not too close.

This is what it feels like.

I wish he were closer.

I wish he were closer than millimeters. I wish he were closer than myself.

I clear my throat. "I think that was my attempt at a pirate, maybe."

"I feel like a pirate. Absconding with my treasure!"

"Wait. Am I the treasure in this metaphor?"

He looks at me. Those goddamn eyes. It's like there's an

alien heart-killing death ray in there. A state secret. "Yes."

This is what it feels like.

Like I'm light and there is nothing holding me down and there is no such thing as time. Time hasn't even been invented.

The boat starts to float its way down the river, and above us, the lights come up on Saint Basil's Cathedral, those red onion spires up into the lavender sky.

And I wish this boat could keep floating up the river forever, up to the Volga, past Yaroslavl, through the waters of the czars to Saint Petersburg, and there we would make a mad dash to Finland and no one would ever know where we are or who we are or what we did or what we never wanted to do.

35

The Moskva River is floating underneath us while Raynes and I are leaning back taking in the sky and the bobbles on the churches, the tips of the buildings. It's nighttime now, a crescent moon in the sky above us, and the few stars we can see.

"Look, there's the Big Dipper. See that?"

Raynes nods, appreciating the entire canvas.

"And there, there's Orion's Belt! Do you see! The three stars there?"

"And what is that there, do you know?"

"That? That is Orion's Sweater Vest."

Raynes turns to me. Leans in.

"What a big discovery. I had no idea Orion's Sweater Vest existed."

"Oh, it exists. It's just rare to see it. Like you have to be on a boat, in the Moskva River, with someone named Paige."

"Oh, thank God I found that last part."

I blush and try to keep everything in joke territory.

"No. Really. Thank God I found that last part."

And this is it, ladies and gentlemen, the moment Sean Raynes, international man of mystery, leans down and actually kisses me.

And the world stops.

I mean, I'm pretty sure it's going on outside our heads. I'm pretty sure the earth is still turning and the moon is still shining and the river is still lapping under the boat beneath us. I'm pretty sure the world hasn't actually stopped turning on its axis. But here. Here in this moment. With this kiss, this kiss that keeps lasting, we might as well be part of the constellations. Just lift us between Andromeda and Pegasus and Ursa Major. Just keep us there.

Forever.

36

Katerina is still up when I get back to the dorm. She's reading *Sula*, by Toni Morrison, underneath a dim clip lamp. My dim clip lamp.

"Wait. Isn't that my lamp?"

"Yes. I like."

"That's a really good novel, by the way."

"Yes, it is about friendship."

She says this in a loaded way, adding, "Between girls."

I stand there for a second, not knowing what to say. Wait. Does she know I'm a spy? Have I been "made," as they say in every Scorsese movie?

"You should also try *Song of Solomon*—that's good, too," I say in an attempt to deflect.

"Maybe." She closes the book. "Can I ask question?"

"Yes, you can ask question."

"Are you falling in love right now?"

"What? No! No, of course not. What would give you that idea? Who would I even fall in love with?"

Katerina contemplates the blue chipped walls a moment.

"I am not sure. Maybe you tell me. Maybe we have girl talk."

"Really? Can we have a pillow fight after?"

"Is that what American girls do?"

"Definitely not. It's sort of like the male idea of what girls do. But it has no basis in reality. Sort of like everything else you see in the media."

"Are all American girls like this?"

"Like what?"

"Like you. Against system."

"Probably more than you would think."

"When I think of American girl, I think of bunny rabbit."

"Do I seem like a bunny rabbit to you, Katerina?"

"Yes. And I am worried about you."

The dim clip lamp is the only thing lighting up our suddenly intimate discourse. I'd turn on the overheads, but they're first-class mood killers.

"Worried about *me*? Seriously?"

"Paige, you are good girl inside. You are kind person. But this is Russia. This is not place for bunny rabbit."

She takes me in, trying not to say too much.

"Maybe there are danger around you don't even realize."

This is a warning. But it's protective, not threatening.

"Katerina, I didn't just fall off the cabbage truck."

"What truck?"

"It's an expression. It means like someone who is over their head, ignorant."

"But why cabbage truck?"

"I don't know why cabbage truck."

"Cabbage truck sound like good place for bunny rabbit."

And, with that, she turns off my stolen clip light and plunges us both into darkness.

37

Uri has invited Katerina and me to lunch. To meet his parents. Actually, just his dad and his dad's trophy girlfriend. You remember her, Queen Elsa? What I don't know is that though I've never met them, they've seen me before.

We are in the sky-blue-and-gold Baroque dining room with white Louis Catorce chairs and a giant ornate Tiffany-blue dome up above. I'm trying hard not to seem like a provincial American and spend the whole time gawking at the scenery.

Now, keep in mind, I have never been here before and I have never met these guys before. You've met them, because I was nice enough to show you that videotape. But right now, at this point in our little ditty, I, Paige Nolan, have no actual idea who these people are or what they are up to. I'm like an innocent little lamb in this scenario. Which makes it a very rare kind of scenario.

"You are long way from home, no?"

Uri's dad, aka Dimitri, aka head honcho kingpin of Moscow, is addressing little ol' me.

"Um, yeah, I guess."

"It is always *I guess* with you Americans. Everything is always *kind of* or *sort of* . . . never defined. Never strong."

"I think it's just our way of being polite, maybe?"

"Yes, so polite while you drop bombs on children. Sorry. While you *kind of* drop bombs on children."

"If you're looking for me to make a positive argument about dropping bombs on civilians, trust me, you've asked the wrong person to lunch. I am absolutely, positively anti-war, anti-imperialism, and a pacifist above everything else. *Nam-myoho-renge-kyo.* That's my Buddhist chant. But sometimes I chant in Aramaic. *Maranatha.* Which means *come, Lord* or *the Lord is coming.* It really depends on how I'm feeling that day."

Dimitri takes this in.

Queen Elsa blows smoke in my face.

Suddenly, Dimitri blurts out. "This is what I don't understand about USA! You have government that does horrible things, or lets horrible things happen all over the world, in client state, in puppet state. Then you meet USA people. And they are like puppy dog."

Queen Elsa blows another drag at me. I don't think she likes me.

"To what do you attribute this discrepancy?"

"Respectfully, sire, Americans are good people."

Look at me. I'm practically Abigail Adams over here! Nothing like a bunch of homeland bashing to make you wave the good ol' red, white, and blue.

"And what do good people think of big traitor Sean Raynes?"

That's weird. Why is he bringing that up? I mean, I guess he's famous and everything . . . ?

"Well. I think he's a hero." I don't tell him he's my almost-boyfriend. "It's just the establishment that hates him."

"Of course. He show the world they are hypocrite."

"Well, this is light conversation over borscht." Uri makes a joke. I think he's actually being protective of me. Sweet.

We all share a fake laugh . . . and then something strange happens.

In the corner, next to an enormous floor-to-ceiling gilded mirror, there is a giant clanking sound.

Everybody at the table, I mean everybody, turns to face the sound, ready to strike. Dimitri. Katerina. Ice Queen.

And Underling. Who points his gun. At the busboy.

But it was only an accident. The busboy dropped a wine-glass while cleaning it. The sound echoes up into the blue sky dome ceiling, reverberating back down in the cavernous space.

The busboy meekly puts his hands up in the air, terrified. "Sorry . . ."

Everyone breathes a sigh of relief.

I can't help but notice Uri and I were the only people *not* to jump.

Interesting.

"Wow. Nervous table." I smile.

Dimitri politely smiles back but is really not amused.

"It was nice to meet you, American Paige. And you, Katerina. We see you soon."

And at that, Dimitri, in all his bald glory, curtly stands up, followed by Underling and Queen Elsa. She gives a look back to the table. Possibly a sneer.

There's a long pause as Katerina, Uri, and I contemplate the interaction.

"They seem nice."

That's my way of breaking the tension.

Katerina rolls her eyes and we all start laughing.

Uri calls over to the busboy, "Hey, busboy who almost got

killed over glass. Come. Bring vodka. And food!"

The busboy looks around and scurries off, presumably to retrieve said vodka.

"Um, Uri, why did your dad want to meet us anyway? I mean, not that we're not fabulous, interesting women of the world. But, seriously? Why? That was kind of weird. All he did was grill me about America. We didn't even eat!"

"Maybe he is writing paper." Katerina smirks.

"Were you just born with that smirk on your face?" I joke. "Like when you came out into the world, did you just sneer at the doctors and ask for a cigarette?"

"Maybe. I ask Mother."

Yes, I know Katerina is a spy. And to be honest, I kind of resent that she's pretending to be my friend. But I can't show it. The best way to cover is to just act normal. Keep it easy breezy, lemon squeezy.

The busboy comes back with a bottle of vodka and three shot glasses.

"No, no. You have one, too," Uri tells the busboy. "I insist. It is not every day you drop wine glass and almost die."

Uri is basically the opposite of his dad, I see.

The bus boy smiles and takes a shot, grateful.

Uri watches him drink the shot and put the glass down. Silence.

"That was poison glass."

The busboy goes white.

"I kid! Kidding!"

The busboy breathes a sigh of relief. Uri and Katerina laugh out loud, a broad, bawdy laugh.

Katerina turns to me.

"You see, American Paige? Russians are nice people, too."

38

Whoever put together Raynes's little pied-à-terre in Moscow I am going to assume didn't want him to leave. I mean, it's stunning. It sits at the top of an extremely modern glass sky-scraper and it has a pool. Not, oh, there's a pool you can go down to share with everyone else. No, there's a pool on the balcony. *Your* balcony. Yep. A private infinity pool on the balcony so it looks like, if you're swimming in the pool, that you could just swim off into the sky.

And I just can't.

Right now Raynes and I are sitting by the pool, under a patio heater cranking full blast, eating sushi and drinking hot sake. Apparently, the pool is heated, in case you were thinking about going for a dip. But it's brisk. Remember, we're on the fourteenth floor.

Don't worry. Oleg is inside, at the kitchen bar, sitting there like a grumpy bug on a toadstool.

"I wouldn't have pictured you in a place like this."

"Me either." Raynes looks embarrassed. "I didn't really have much choice."

A breeze blows across the deck.

"How bad is it?"

"What?"

"Your kind of superglamorous captivity."

"It's surreal. I mean. They won't send me back. Because Putin enjoys humiliating America so much. And they won't kill me. For two reasons. Number one, that becomes an international incident between the US and Russia. New cold war. Not good. And number two . . . they know I have more information. Maybe something they want. Maybe something they can use against the States. If I die, they never find it."

"Whoa!" I say like this is big news to me. "Not to be, like, macabre but . . . couldn't they just get whatever you have by torturing it out of you? Feel free to tell me to stop talking, by the way."

"No, it's a good question. Again, there's two reasons. One, that's back to an international incident, and two"—he stops, glances around, lowers his voice—"what I have, if I'm killed, goes out anyway. I actually designed a program that gets set off if they kill me. Or if anybody kills me. And, of course, they know that, too."

"Ah! So *that's* why you're still alive. Well, I'm happy to hear it. I really prefer to hang out with live people."

We clink sake cups, in a devil-may-care kind of cheers, and I think for a second.

"Wait. Can't they just hack you? I mean, I'm sure they've got all their best guys trying to figure out how to hack everything you've ever remotely taken an interest in. Trying to find where it's embedded?"

"That is what *they* would assume, isn't it?"

Okay, I have to lay off before he starts to get suspicious.

But I can't resist just one teensy-weensy last question.

"So do you?"

"What?"

"Have, you know, additional somethings? Somethings someone would really want?"

He smiles.

"Wouldn't you like to know."

Oleg turns on the TV inside.

I squint at Raynes. "I feel like pushing you in the pool right now."

"You would never push me in the pool right now."

"Why, do you think Oleg would jump in and throw me off the building?"

"Maybe. He's very possessive."

I stand up to peek at Oleg. It looks like he's watching some sort of heist movie. Raynes and I stand side by side, taking him in.

"Do you think he's pissed he's got this duty? To watch you?"

"I can't tell. He's impenetrable. It's like talking to a building."

And then I push him.

Yes! Ladies and gentlemen, Paige Nolan has just pushed public enemy number one into the swimming pool. In his clothes.

There's only one problem.

Right when he's about to fall backward, he reaches out and grabs my sleeve, which grabs my arms, and then, of course, takes all of me into the heated (thank God, heated!) swimming pool. Fourteen stories up. On a skyscraper in Moscow. The lights of the city all around us.

"You satanist!" I splash him.

"You strumpet!" Now his turn.

"You scoundrel!" Now me.

"You soul-sucker!!" We are splashing each other like five-year-olds only to look up and see Oleg glowering down at us from the edge of the pool.

Why do I feel busted?

"Everything's all right, Oleg! Just *splashin' around!*"

I laugh at this last part. Such a dork.

Oleg is not amused.

He returns back to the living room, nonplussed.

"He's a real people person," I whisper to Raynes.

But it doesn't matter what I just said because Raynes has just now attacked me. With his mouth.

Under the stars and the lights of Moscow.

It is the best attack.

39

Okay, busted.

I spent the night.

Listen, don't judge me. I am not just totally enraptured with a certain someone who shall remain nameless, but I am doing this out of a duty for my country. I am *sacrificing* here, okay?

And no. I'm not going to tell you all the slurpy details.
Pervert.

All I'm going to say is this . . . When I think about this night, even now and probably forevermore, I will have to stop whatever I'm doing and stand still and catch my breath and try to compose myself.

So that's all you get to know.

Quit it.

It's about four in the morning, and I am perfecting my walk-of-shame tiptoe scheme when I notice a copy of *The Painted Bird* on the bookshelf.

Hey! That's kind of nifty. Our book! That's our book! It's a sign!

Then I look closer and I realize there's something sticking out of the top of it. Like a postcard or a picture or a receipt.

I tiptoe over, not wanting to wake Raynes, and oh-so-gently take the book down to look at the photo. It's not a postcard, after all—it's just a printed screenshot. I can see the settings bar at the top of the picture.

Strange.

The picture is of a round little mud structure with a wooden door, a giant red rock formation the size of a building behind it, and a vast sunset desert sky. Everything in the picture is glowing a kind of pink sienna. Shimmering.

"Um. What are you doing?"

Whoops.

Busted.

I really didn't mean to wake him up, but now there he is, in all his scruffy, raven-haired glory, squinting at me.

"Oh, um . . . sorry, I just saw you had *The Painted Bird*, and I picked it up and this fell out."

So, basically, I was snooping around.

Ugh. Sorry.

"Oh yeah. Cool, thanks." He grabs the picture from me *really* fast. Like he nabs it away.

"What a beautiful picture . . ."

I'm trying to ease the tension. It's so not working.

"Oh. Yeah. Thanks."

Okay, this is really bad. He seems . . . annoyed?

"Why are you leaving so early? Don't you want to stay? I could make you eggs or something."

Wait. Is *that* why he's annoyed? He thought I was ghosting on him? Not the snooping part?

"I—I didn't—"

"I honestly think it's kind of rude of you to just leave. You didn't even say good-bye or anything."

Oh.

Okay.

Quite frankly, I'm pretty sure my bachelors back home were relieved by my disappearing act. Not disappointed.

So this is new.

"I guess I just figured it'd kind of be better not to have to make awkward conversation and feel stupid and insecure."

"Come here. Let's make awkward conversation and feel stupid and insecure *together*. How about that?"

"Is that, like, a demand, like an I'm-the-man-so-I-decide kind of demand?"

"No, it's a demand like, please don't leave. I don't want you to go."

"Oh. All right, I won't."

A smile breaks on his face like a kid who's just caught sight of his Christmas loot. "Cool. Now how do you like your eggs?"

"Like my disposition."

"Scrambled?"

I swat at him. "I was going to say sunny side up."

But, scrambled . . . truer words have never been spoken.

40

I'm two steps from home on my walk of shame when it hits me.

Madden is half-asleep when I get him over my hot red Beats connection.

"Speak."

"I need a ticket back to the States."

"What? Why?"

"I think I know where Raynes is keeping the whatever-he-has."

He yawns. "Okay, fine. But you better be right."

"I am. I'm right. I know I'm right."

Suddenly, the picture pops in my head of my parents,

there in that dusty complex in the middle of God knows where.

I have to be right.

I'm going to be right.

41

It takes me about a day to get there, with the plane, then the second plane, which is the little plane, then the car, which is a rental.

I try my hardest during this extended transport not to think about the possibility I have no idea what I am doing.

Let's be honest. I'm basically operating off a hunch.

But it's like this.

I have feels for Raynes. As much as I hate that. As much as I'd rather not admit it. There's something there. There's a *connection*, like I've known him a lot longer than I have. Like we've met before or something. Like we're remeeting each other.

And maybe that time before was a hundred years ago or a

thousand years ago or never. Maybe it's just me being stupid. But I feel like I know him, what's inside him, what makes him tick. Because I know me. What's inside me. What makes me tick. And I'm pretty sure it's the same.

That's why I think I'm right.

About my hunch.

He told that Navajo story, remember? About Fortress Rock? It means something to him. The Navajo. Their rebellion. Their refusal to go quietly into the night. They didn't do what they were supposed to do. What the army wanted them to do. What the US wanted them to do.

Kind of like him.

And, in the end, they were vindicated.

They won.

They were right.

They were enemies who, after a time, were celebrated as heroes.

The second thing is this. Raynes acted distinctly un-Raynes-like, unnatural, and even a little bit scared when he saw me staring at that picture. The screenshot. Quite frankly, he lost his cool. And he put a wall up. It was brief. He recovered. But initially, he was defensive. He was defending something.

And I think I know what he was defending.

It took me a while, using the magic of the internet, to

figure out what exactly I was looking at in that screenshot.

And yes, when he went into the other room, I grabbed my phone and took a picture of the screenshot. So now I have a screenshot of a screenshot. Very meta.

So, that round mud building in the photo, according to the interbot, is a "round dwelling; with or without internal posts; timber or stone walls and packed with earth in varying amounts or a bark roof for a house, with the door facing east to welcome the rising sun for wealth and good fortune."

It is called a hogan.

And it is the primary traditional dwelling of one tribe.

They call themselves the Diné.

But there is a name that we, the white man, have given them . . .

which is . . .

the Navajo.

42

Monument Valley Navajo Tribal Park.

That's where it is. That enormous red tower sticking out of the ground, looking out across the mesa. That's in Monument Valley. It's so distinct, sticking up out of the earth with one, thinner spire on the side, it has a name. West Mitten Butte.

Makes sense.

It does look like a mitten.

This is one of those places you see for the first time and don't understand why you were dumb enough not to come sooner. The luminous, pink light off the red rocks and mesas, the bright azure sky like it was painted, all of it makes you feel like there has to be a God. There just must be. To make this.

Wherever this place is, this Navajo hogan, this rock in the photo, West Mitten Butte, is somewhere behind it. Probably pretty far judging by the size. The good news is, there aren't that many roads. The bad news is, there's no guarantee this hogan is near any roads. It's kind of like looking for a needle in a haystack. This place is bigger than it looks in the picture.

Not that I mind it, though.

This is the exact opposite of being in an underground supper club in Moscow. It's vast and stunning and there's no one around for miles. And that's not all. There's something else here, too. Almost like a spirit. You feel like someone is watching over you, but not in a creepy way. You feel like there's something in the air, a sort of kindness, enveloping you.

I don't understand it.

I really don't. But I can see why this is hallowed land. Why it holds a special place to the Navajo, why it's considered the heart of the earth. Sacred.

This is the place Raynes stashed his trump card. I can feel it.

If I look at this screenshot, there's only one butte in

the background. But when I look at the map there are two nearby, forming a kind of triangle. East Mitten Butte and Merrick's Butte. Neither of these are in the picture. But judging by where the one spire comes up from the rock, the finger of the mitten, and knowing that the door of the hogan must face east, I can begin to approximate where this fateful place must be. And it's not near the road.

Glad I brought some water.

If I don't make it back by sunset, you can just spread my ashes here. Promise?

43

It takes me about four hours, off the trail, to find it.

There, essentially hidden, camouflaged against the mesa, is the abandoned hogan. There's nothing around it for miles. Not a shed, not another dwelling, not a human being. Just this structure, with a wooden door facing east.

Thank goodness it's fall, otherwise I'm sure I wouldn't have made it. As it is, though, it's the perfect easy, breezy temperature for me to not die after a four-hour hike.

I stand there for a moment, taking it in, a breeze coming over the mesa.

Suddenly, I feel like I'm trespassing. Like I'm violating this sacred place in this sacred land where I have no business.

I look up to the sky.

"I'm sorry."

I don't exactly know who I'm talking to—maybe the wind. But whatever the case may be, I feel like there's a respect I have to have. In this place. This place that's watching me.

I approach with reverence and caution. After all, this is rattlesnake city. Scorpion central. I push the door open. No bites or stings. Yet.

If you've never been inside a hogan, I'll give you a clue. It's a little bit like being inside an upside-down wicker basket. The entire inside is a series of interlocking thin rectangular logs, intricately placed to keep the thing standing up. Then the mud part goes outside of that. So . . . on the inside, it's actually really beautiful. You really wouldn't think it would look like this. Throw in a couple of rugs and you could Airbnb this place for $300 a night. YOUR OWN NAVAJO HOGAN IN MONUMENT VALLEY!! LET YOUR TROU-BLES SLIP AWAY!!!

Yes, all caps.

It takes me only about three hours to cover every milli-meter of every inch of every piece of wood, twig, dirt, and a few spiders in here.

Three hours and guess what I come up with.

That's right.

Nothing.

Goose egg.

Zilch.

God, I'm such a loser. What's happening now is I am kind of bumping my head over and over on the side of the hogan wall.

"Idiot. I'm an idiot. Why am I such an idiot?"

What was I thinking? I *understand* Raynes? Raynes cares about the Navajo people? I've known him for, like, six weeks. What the hell do I know? Am I insane?

The worst part is Madden.

I'm gonna have to tell Madden just how much I suck.

Hey, remember that total hunch I randomly went on and made you send me on an emergency spiritual journey from Moscow to Monument Valley that must have cost a giant chunk of change? Well, I was kind of wrong about that whole thing. Sorry.

Ugh.

I bump my head against the hogan a little too hard.

Ouch. Jesus. How delusional am I?

I'm exhausted and exasperated and humiliated. I take a moment to lie on the ground and admit defeat.

Failed.

I have failed.

44

Twenty minutes later, my heart jumps.

Just like that.

It jumps, and I am up on my feet and out the door.

I grab the screenshot of the screenshot from my pocket and start walking.

It's about two hundred feet to where the picture was taken.

I turn around and hold up the picture.

Back up.

Back up more . . .

There.

There. That's it.

Do you see that? Right here, right here in this spot? If I

hold it up, this is it. The exact place where the picture was taken. The POV of the picture, if you will. And you will.

Without knowing what I'm doing or even why, I just start digging. Right at my feet, not stopping, no dwelling, just going for it.

It's getting harder, so I use a stick and a kind of pointy rock and whatever else I can find to keep it up. I don't ask why, I'm just propelled into this, possessed.

It's about twenty minutes in when I hit something.

I stop.

Put the rock down, look inside the dirt, squint.

I brush the dirt off whatever it is.

Could be a rock.

Maybe even a bone.

Who knows.

But as I dust it off I realize.

It's neither.

No, no.

Ladies and gentlemen, it is . . .

A very ancient, Native American . . . flash drive.

45

Have you ever seen a girl dancing by herself in the middle of Monument Valley next to a hogan? I haven't either. But that's what I'm doing. Shaking. And jumping. Lots of jumping.

"I did it! I did it! YAAAAAAASSSSS! Hell yeah! Yes yes yes yes yes!"

And now I fall to my knees.

"Thank you. Thank you thank you thank you. Whoever or whatever just did that. Thank you."

I am so happy, giddy, elated, and all those other words that describe something no one ever is. I am beside myself. Or on top of myself or something.

I feel like my feet are about three feet off the ground.

And I get to feel that way for about two minutes.

Two minutes of pure ecstasy until I am knocked to the earth.

Literally.

46

You know those old-timey cartoons, from back in the *Looney Tunes* days, when someone would get hit and they'd hear Tweety Birds and see stars circling around them? I never really got that. Until now.

Because *I'm* hearing Tweety Birds and seeing stars circling all around the outskirts of my skull.

Something, or some*one*, hit me really hard.

I never even saw it coming.

I really didn't.

When I finally catch my bearings and focus, I realize I am staring up at the bright blue cloudless sky. For an instant I think, am I in heaven? Then I remember, no, I am not in heaven. I am in Monument Valley.

Close. But no cigar.

Around me I can hear nothing.

The Tweety Birds have finally quieted down.

I sit up, dust myself off, and try to acclimate myself.

Okay.

I *had* something.

There was a thing that I had.

I'd been looking for it.

What was it?

It was right here.

Oh yes.

The flash drive!

Oh God.

I lost the flash drive!

Wait, no. I didn't lose the flash drive. That's not what happened. Someone took the flash drive. Someone smashed me in the head and took the flash drive.

Out here.

In the middle of nowhere.

I look around me. Nothing for miles and miles across the mesa. And now to the east. Nothing for miles and miles. West?

Nothing.

Except.

Wait.

What is that?

There. Do you see it?

Halfway down the horizon. I see it. A figure. A person. A person walking. Not running or anything. But walking pretty fast. I can see the red dust coming up behind them.

And I can't tell who it is.

They're too far.

Halfway across the mesa to the road.

Halfway between East Mitten Butte and Merrick's Butte.

Well, I guess I better do something about that.

I sigh.

I guess I did my victory dance prematurely.

I'm a third of the way to the road, with the sun coming up across the mesa, hyperventilating because I've never run so fast in my entire life, when I realize that the figure walking away from me, the figure who followed me from Timbuktu to the middle of nowhere, the figure who clocked me and took the flash drive and is planning on taking it to God knows where is . . .

Katerina.

47

I know you think because I am an international superspy I am going to now take out my supersonic, double-secret laser blaster and evaporate Katerina into smithereens.

And I would like to tell you that's what I do.

But it's not.

By the time Katerina notices I'm running after her at quadruple my normal speed, she's almost to the main road. And, of course, she takes off.

I don't know how fast she is, but if her karate moves are any indication, she's faster than me.

So, I do what any self-respecting outrun, outchopped person would do.

I throw a rock at her head.

I know, I know.

High-tech.

But it works.

I guess all that archery practice at supersecret spy school actually worked. I never would have thought I could hit a moving target from this far away. I make up my mind not to tell Madden he had a positive effect on my life.

But desperation might have helped here.

And adrenaline—that might have helped, too.

Katerina hits the ground, and I bet now she's the one hearing Tweety Birds.

I take off toward her, hoping she doesn't recover, because if she gets up I am screwed AF. Remember, she's got that Death Star belt. They probably had her doing karate kicks in day care.

When I get to her, she's still on the ground. She's not dead, though, praise the gods. She's sort of just lolling around. I guess that rock hit her pretty hard.

"Sorry. I'm so sorry. Sorry."

I grab the flash drive out of her pocket.

She rolls her head over to me. Squinting into the sun, behind my back.

"American Paige. You cannot leave me here."

"It's okay. I'll call nine-one-one. And, by the way, how the hell did you find me?"

"I track headphones."

"Aw, Jesus. Are you serious? You knew about the head-phones? Okay, stay here. Don't make me throw any more rocks at you."

"I can't see out of eye."

"That's okay. That's okay, they're going to be able to fix it. We have the best hospitals in the world. By the way, do you have health insurance?"

"You are joking."

"Okay, we'll cross that bridge when we come to it. I gotta go."

I'm five steps away before I turn and walk back over to her.

"Here. Here's my water. It's important to stay hydrated."

She nods a delirious nod, and I take off to the car.

I'm just past Merrick's Butte when I call 911 and throw my red Beats out the window.

48

My exhilarated sense of freedom after cutting the cord and throwing out my red Beats is extremely short-lived.

Like humiliatingly so.

This place, the Dover Motel, looks not unlike the motel in *Psycho* but with a little more flair and panache. The neon sign above the awning has one letter that blinks on and off. Dover Motel. Over Motel. Dover Motel. Over Motel. And so on and so on, into the dusty, transcendent desert eternity.

No electronic key cards here. Here it's just an old-fashioned silver key on a green plastic ring. Old-school.

Except that I guess it makes it pretty easy to break in.

Why, you ask?

Oh, because Madden is sitting right there on the blue-and-red flowered bedspread when I open the door.

Behind him, there's a painting on the wall of a coyote howling at the moon.

49

"Nice digs."

"I thought it was cool in an ironic kind of way."

"I think it's cool in a bedbugs kind of way."

"I'm actually thinking of asking them if I can buy that painting behind you. The one of the coyote."

"Really? Would you like to put it next to your prized piece of dogs playing poker?"

"I don't have dogs playing poker. That's just too on the nose."

"Of course."

"I bet you're wondering if I have saved the world or failed completely in my primary mission as an international super-spy."

"I am, indeed, wondering that."

"I almost feel like making you wait because you're clearly so excited."

"I'm on tenterhooks."

"You're on Tinder hooks?"

"Very amusing. Now, Paige, I know this is all very thrilling, sitting in the catbird seat and all that . . . but time is of the essence, and that is the only reason I am sitting here in the middle of this rat-infested lice camp—"

"Is it to confess your love for me?"

"Paige. C'mon."

"Okay, okay. Close your eyes. Are they closed? Now . . . put out your hand . . . Don't peek. Ready. There. Now open."

Madden opens his eyes and sees the dusty flash drive in his palm.

The entirety of his face lights up in disbelief.

"No."

"Yes."

"It can't be."

"Yes, it is. It is. I found it! I effing figured it out! Because I . . . used my spider sense."

"Okay, Paige. What's on here?"

"I don't know! We have to plug it in."

I reach out to grab my laptop, but Madden stops me.

"No! We can't do that here. Are you crazy?"

"Crazy?"

"Yes! It is not a good idea to open up a flash drive from a known superhacker, computer genius, public enemy number one, in a motel, on an open server."

"Oh. Right."

"Just give it to me. I'll take care of it."

"Okay, but it behooves you to tell me what's on it, considering that I found it through what can only be considered an extraordinary perception, possibly extraterrestrial in its proportions."

"So now you're an alien? Honestly, Paige. I wouldn't be surprised."

"Also, someone, probably an FSB spy, followed me here, followed me out into the middle of the desert, knocked me out, and tried to take off with the flash drive."

Madden looks actually surprised.

No, I don't tell him it was Katerina. And I don't know why I don't tell him. I'll figure out that part of my unbalanced personality later.

"How did they find you?"

"Who knows?! *Probably* those stupid red Beats you gave me. I mean, maybe they tracked them? You're lucky I'm so wily as to catch up with said FSB spy, defeat said FSB spy, and get back the flash drive."

"And how, exactly, did you *defeat* said FSB spy, Paige?"

"It's too complicated for you even to understand."

I don't tell him that I lobbed a rock at her. I simply shrug. The embodiment of humility.

"Well, regardless. Well done, Paige. But you should change hotels. Not just because this place is teeming with vermin but, also, because whoever they are, they probably know you're here. In fact, they're probably coming here right now. Which is why I'm leaving."

"That's good. I was getting a little uncomfortable with you sitting on the bed this whole time. Have you ever seen what's on those bedspreads in that special spooky CSI light? Terrifying."

Madden gets up. "Well, as usual, it's been weird."

He heads out the door.

"Don't forget, switch motels. Actually, try a hotel. Honestly, you've earned it. We'll take care of the bill."

"Really? Can I add in, like, a spa treatment?"

"Don't press your luck."

"Just asking."

Then he throws something on the bed. "By the way, you're famous."

He walks out, leaving me with the *Moscow Times*. There. At the bottom of the page. Is a picture of Raynes and me strolling along the river, making goo-goo eyes at each other. Looking very much in love. It appears Oleg was cut out of the picture. The headline reads "An American Affair." Not bad, but I think they could've done something more dramatic. I would have chosen "An American in Moscow" or "Love on Red Square" or maybe "Kremlin Nights: Love Fast, Die Young." Below said tepid headline is a story about Paige Nolan, American foreign exchange student and sweetheart of world-renowned CIA buster Sean Raynes.

This fills me with a sense of glee, confusion, pride, insecurity, shame, affection, and fear. These sentiments all just rotate in a circle around my head for the next five hours, in the path laid by the Tweety Birds, each of them showing up in different forms to hound me on a kind of Ferris wheel of emotion.

Ah, the feels!

50

This place is fancy. Not fancy in the hey-we-were-all-born-on-the Mayflower sort of way. No, no. Fancy in the we-are-so-rich-we-are-Bohemian kind of way. So even though it's three hundred dollars a night for a *standard* room, there's all sorts of Navajo rugs and spiritual stylings in every crag of every corner. For instance, above my bed is a dream catcher. I wonder if it will catch my dreams about Gael García Bernal deciding that he is in love with me.

Right now I'm in a sandstone tubby with eucalyptus bubble bath bubbles up to my eyebrows. This is my favorite way to be. I can fantasize about disappearing under the water and reappearing under the sea. All my friends will be sea creatures with different personalities based on their species.

My crab friend will always be crabby. My shark friend will always be sly. My BFF dolphin friend will always be trying to trick me into playful shenanigans. We will be happy there under the sea. We'll sing and splash and frolic in the coral reef. Every once in a while a family of whales will migrate past us and we'll stop to listen to their eerie, beautiful whale songs. We'll shun humans. Whenever humans or boats are anywhere near us, we'll call them "flat feet" and hide and giggle and make fun of them. Such will be life under the sea!

But my phone rings and that all goes away.

Good-bye, sea creatures—we were good together!

It's Madden.

"What?"

"Meet me downstairs."

"I can't. I'm in the bathtub daydreaming."

"Paige, come downstairs."

"My sea creature name will be Lobstertails."

"Paige!"

"Okay, fine."

It's funny, this moment. I didn't realize it at the time. But this moment, here, in the bath, fantasizing about life at the bottom of the ocean, was kind of like my way of ending it. This spy adventure. Everybody go back to what you were doing. Everything is fine. Done. Over.

Which is to say, I was entirely kidding myself.

51

The desert-themed hotel bar at this place is pretty generic. Lots of sienna and even a few multicolored pebble fountains. But there's a wall of windows looking over Monument Valley in the distance, so that's really the draw.

Madden is sitting down at a two-top, looking serious.

(That's restaurant lingo from when I worked as a waitress.)

(For one week.)

(Yes, they fired me.)

(I couldn't remember anyone's orders because, well, because I didn't care.)

"By the way, if you are interested in turquoise jewelry, you may want to visit the hotel gift shop, which has offerings that consist almost entirely of turquoise jewelry. And cedar-scented candles."

"Paige. Sit down."

He doesn't even smile.

Usually, I can get at least the beginnings of a smirk.

"What?"

"I have some news for you, and it's probably going to be hard for you to take, but I'm hoping you won't make a scene."

"Make a scene? What, are you breaking up with me?"

"Paige. This is serious."

He sighs and looks out the plateglass window over the red stone rock formations, placed like dominoes, in the distance.

"The flash drive. The one you so remarkably found . . . it's a list."

"A list?"

"Yes. It's a list of names. Of RAITH operatives. All of them, all over the world, in over one hundred different countries, some of which are extremely unfriendly to us."

"What do you mean?"

"That's his plan. Raynes. To release the list."

"Wait. What? Why? Why would he do that?"

"Because we think he believes that RAITH, with all its secret civilian operatives and congressional unaccountability, is a violation of the Constitution. He believes the rogue nature of RAITH is a danger to our democracy, operating even more secretly and undercover than both the CIA and the FBI. That's why."

"So, wait, how many people are on the list?"

"Thousands."

This does not compute. Raynes is an *Elliott Smith fan*. If his security was compromised, he wouldn't take out thousands of people. Right? "You're about to say you're making this up—"

"Paige, if this gets out, people could die. Horrible deaths. Not just executions. Torture. It will be a field day for all of our enemies, capturing our operatives, extracting state secrets."

"He wouldn't do that. Raynes. He would never do that."

"Paige, it's all there. If he's killed, a program is tripped. He checks in twice a day. If he stops checking in, because, say, he's dead, the program launches and the info is sent on how to find the flash drive. It's like a treasure hunt for nerds. And once they finish their little nerd hunt and find the flash drive, it'll be front-page news. But not anymore, Paige. The fact that you found the flash drive first is a miracle. Now we just have to pray that Raynes doesn't know we're on to him and release the information himself. That is, if we thought praying would help."

"Wait. You don't believe in God?"

He shrugs. "Jury's out. Why? Do you?"

"Well, I've just never met anyone happy who doesn't believe in *something*."

I shrug it off, but, by the way, in my experience, that is 100 percent true.

I need to disentangle myself from this entire mess. My mission was to find out what Raynes was hiding. I did that. So, time for my exit.

"So, I'm done now, right? I did my job. Successfully, I might add, and I can go home. And we can figure out our next move vis-à-vis my parents once this situation is all cleaned up. Yes?"

"Not quite."

"No. Just stop talking."

Madden leans in.

"The list. Only he knows where he embedded the list online. There's no more analog, you see? You just took away his only backup. Do you understand? That flash drive was the only thing keeping him alive. Now it's just him."

"Jesus. So I just took away his life support."

"Correct."

"Look, you never told me that was—"

"Paige, nobody knew what he had, or where he had it. That was the mission."

"Right. And now that the mission is complete, I'm not

going back to Moscow. No way. FSB already must know I'm an operative." And they'll definitely know I'm an operative once Katerina explains how she got that concussion.

"Maybe. But if they didn't kill you by now, they're not going to kill you. You have to go back," Madden repeats.

"No, I don't."

"Paige, listen to me. You have a new assignment."

"No, sorry. I'm done. I passed with flying colors, and now I'm done."

He stares at me, and I can see the indecision on his face. Should he say what he's going to say next? I shake my head in a barely perceptible signal that no, he shouldn't.

Regardless, he leans in.

"They want you to kill him."

"What? Fuck no!"

I don't tell him, but he has to know that I am kinda, sorta developing feelings for Raynes even though I never do that except with hypothetical people like Gael García Bernal.

"It's a direct order."

"I don't care. I'm not doing it. There's nothing in the world that could make me do that."

"You're the only one close enough to him *to* do it. You're the only one who can slip by FSB radar to do it. And the clock is ticking. If that FSB agent out in the desert told them about the flash drive, which I'm certain he did, they're piecing it together right now. They could take Raynes in. Torture him for the information on that flash drive, then kill him. You have to leave for Moscow tonight."

"I said I'm not doing it."

He presses his lips together so they form a thin line. "They'll send someone else. You know that. Someone to whom Raynes is just a mark." He's giving me this look now. A deep, intense stare into my eyes. He's trying to tell me something without saying it. "You're the best person to . . . *navigate this.*"

"Navigate this?" I repeat.

There's something going on underneath this. Maybe some serpentine orders from the executives up above. Whatever it is, Madden seems like more of a messenger right now than a suit.

He gives me a nod. And with that, Madden leaves my plane ticket on the table and walks off.

Outside the plateglass window, the sun turns the mesa blazing orange. Bright as a bomb blast.

INTERLUDE
II

All you have to do is look at the report from that very morning. It's
a doozy. Dallas. Love Field. There's an entire bandstand set up. A
stage. A podium. Red, white, and blue decorations. The picture is
set up perfectly, the stage facing the runway, in the background a
grassy, green field, the distant Dallas skyline, framed by the cloudless bright-blue sky.

Everyone is reportedly there. The sheriff. The mayor. Even the
governor is rumored to be arriving. There are a number of what
look like oilmen in suits and Stetsons—ten-gallon hats. Bolo ties set
in turquoise. Their wives, hair perfectly coiffed, in sundresses. A few
toddlers. A few babies, sleeping in their strollers. A few annoyed boys,
playing cowboys and Indians, asking, when can we go, wheeeeeen
can we GO!? Everyone. For this triumphant announcement, for
this pink pony show. And there is going to be a surprise, boy howdy.

This is going to be on every news stations from Manhattan to Mumbai. Top story.

And everyone is just waiting. Waiting there in the hot, sticky, Texas late afternoon. Waiting. Waving fans. Fanning flies. Looking at one another. Hanging on every word, each new rumor, whispers through the crowd. Shrugging.

They've been waiting there since sunrise.

1

I am really beginning to like watching these videos with you. It's, like, our *thing*.

Plus, there's something vaguely thrilling about being able to go back and piece it all together. Even though I know how it ends, and you don't, there's this feeling I have, each time, of wonder. Each time, picking up on some little tic, some subtle thing I maybe missed before. A clue.

And then there is the mystery of figuring it out. When was this video taken? What was I doing then? Who was involved?

Like this one.

This one here.

I happened to be halfway between the States and Moscow,

at an altitude of thirty-nine thousand feet above sea level, when this video was taken from our favorite blue Baroque gilded restaurant. I am probably snoozing somewhere up in the night sky, passed out on my third vodka tonic, when this happens. Having no idea, no clue, that miles way, a third of the way across the world, a trap is being set.

Dimitri sits at his usual table. Queen Elsa is playing Candy Crush on her iPhone.

Sitting next to Dimitri is our favorite little henchman, Underling. He leans in.

"A little bird tells me that Raynes is fucked."

Dimitri frowns. "Why fucked?"

"He had backup plan, something for his minions, in case he get hurt."

"And?"

Underling smiles. "He no longer has backup plan. The Americans. They discover."

"This is good, yes?"

"It's perfect. It means whatever he has"—Underling points at his head—"he has here. He knows how to find. Encrypted."

Dimitri thinks. "And FSB? Do they know this?"

"Not yet. But when they find out, he is dead. They will find way to make him disappear and torture. He has no chance. He is weak. Pathetic."

Dimitri contemplates the place setting. "What do you think it is? This thing he has."

Underling pretends to think, but it's not his strong suit. "I don't know. But whatever it is . . . must be important. The Americans are going crazy about it."

Dimitri leans back and looks at Ice Queen, who doesn't even look up or acknowledge his existence. After a moment he turns back to Underling.

"We change the minimum. Double the price. One billion. Tell them they have three days. We give him to highest bidder."

Underling nods and turns to leave.

Dimitri contemplates the picture in the newspaper, the one of Raynes and me having a romantic stroll along the banks of the Moskva River.

"One more thing. Get Uri."

He smiles at Ice Queen.

"You see. My idiot son may be useful after all."

She doesn't look up.

2

The first thing I see when I walk into my Moscow dorm room is Katerina, sitting on her bed with her head bandaged, glaring at me. I put my suitcase down in silence and sit on my bed.

The two of us stare at each other for what feels like a century.

"Well, this is awkward."

Katerina just sits there, perfectly content to breathe air so thick you could cut it with a knife.

"Okay, so, in America? When something is really awkward and uncomfortable, we do something totally crazy and weird. We talk about it."

"Talk?"

"Yes, talk. Try it. You'll like it."

"No talk."

"Yes talk."

If it's possible to shrug with your eyes, that's what she does.

I plug my hair dryer into the socket and blast it on high to cover our conversation.

Katerina makes a face. Yes, it is annoying.

"Okay, I'll start, since I'm the more experienced one. So. I know about you. You know about me."

She nods.

"We both know the other one *is a spy*." I whisper that last part.

She nods again.

"Now I didn't tell anyone about you. My question to you is . . . did you tell anyone about me? Just nod. Yes or no?"

Katerina takes me in a second, turning it over in her head.

"*Nyet.*"

"Okay, good. I probably shouldn't believe you, but okay."

She scoffs. "Believe. They just think you are stupid student girl."

"Good. That's good. So, there's three ways to do this . . . one is to kill each other, two is to tell on the other one and maybe get the other one killed, and the last, and my personal preference, is not to tell anyone and live in a kind of purgatorial, Switzerland-like state of mutual feigned ignorance. Oh, and that last way? Everyone gets to stay alive."

Katerina lightens up a bit. "Go on."

"We have the same interests here. Our bosses may not understand it, but we do." I pause. "There's this story in the States. From World War One. In the trenches. I guess the night of Christmas Eve, both the French and the Germans stopped killing each other for once and came out of their trenches and sang Christmas carols and drank whiskey and maybe played soccer. I can't remember. But the important thing is, they suspended their fighting, realizing they were just cogs in a great wheel, fighting a rich man's war, which one can argue has always been—"

"Okay, okay. I get point."

"So, what I'm asking is . . . can we just maybe pretend it's Christmas Eve? In the trenches?"

Katerina contemplates.

She nods. "Christmas Eve."

I breathe a huge sigh of relief. I didn't want to have to rat on anyone before breakfast.

But now Katerina has her own questions . . .

"Tell me. What is on flash drive?"

"I have no idea. It's above my pay grade."

"You're lying, American Paige. Not nice lying during the holidays."

"Look, if it makes you feel any better, I'm done. My assignment. Fin. Over. Mission complete."

"Is that like your George W. Bush with 'Mission Accomplished' banner, playing dress-up in flight suit?"

We share a moment here.

"Now maybe we can go back to our preordained arrangement of cool Russian girl and admiring yet goofy BFF—"

"If you are done, why are you back?"

She raises an eyebrow. And there is that mischievous smile again. Even if I tried to hate her I couldn't. She's not the enemy. She's me on the other side.

And it's Christmas Eve.

Obviously, I'm not about to give her the nuclear codes or anything. But I am definitely not planning on suffocating her in her sleep. And, hopefully, as we just agreed, she's not planning that either.

This Hallmark moment is interrupted by a rap at the door.

No, an actual rap.

And then Uri barges in.

"Go, Uri, it's my birthday. Go, Uri, it's my birthday!"

Katerina and I exchange a look.

"Hello, fly ladies! I invite you to off-the-hook birthday party. It will be mad dope, yo."

"Um, Uri. It's okay to just talk in your normal voice. We're not exactly Salt N Pepa over here."

"Where is party?" Katerina asks.

"That is thing. My dad is throwing for me, at dacha. Will be off the chain. You must come. I insist."

Katerina and I speak at the same time.

"So I was thinking about organizing my—"

"I have made plans with other—"

Then he makes a sort of puppy-dog face.

"Ladygirls. Is important to me."

Katerina and I share a look. Uri notices her bandages.

"What happen to your head?"

"She threw rock at me." She points at me.

"It was an accident. We were playing . . . baseball."

Uri makes a face. Doubtful. Katerina shrugs.

"Oh, and bring boyfriend, American Paige. He will be like celebrity guest. I stand close to him, more girls will like me."

"Boyfriend?"

"Don't play shy. Everyone know you are little American vixen who steal heart of famous traitor. Was in newspaper. You should be happy. You are famous!"

"I didn't peg you as a newspaper reader, Uri."

"Really was on gossip website. Not good picture of you, but I tell friends you are pretty."

"Thanks."

Katerina smiles; she is enjoying this.

"Well, there is one good picture of you. One in passport. But nobody notice that. Mostly you look like, how you say, girl who fell out of trash can."

Now Katerina laughs. At my expense.

"Okay, okay. Enough humiliation. It's hard to live this life under a microscope. But I will ask him. Raynes. About coming to your party. Since your dad is . . . who he is, there will be adequate protection, I assume."

"Enough talk! *I* ask him." Katerina dives for my phone and starts texting.

"What? What are you doing?"

She turns her back to me, hunched over my phone.

Before I know it Katerina has fired off rapid text and response, masquerading as me, to Raynes. She turns back around, smiling a devilish little grin.

"You can have now." She hands me back the phone, non-chalant. "Oh, and he say he'd love to. Never seen dacha."

She winks at Uri.

"Happy birthday. Girls will like you now."

3

Russians don't smile.

No, seriously. I'm not making it up or being bitter or grumpy.

I'm saying that, as a culture, this is a thing.

You know how, if you go to the store and you're checking out . . . you know how the cashier gives you a fake smile at the end? And you give a fake smile back? Or you say, "Thanks," or "Have a nice day!" and then smile? Well, the Russians, they just skip that last part. Or if you see someone on the street, maybe you're walking your dog, and they nod at you? You nod back, and you both do a fake smile? Yeah, no fake smile here. They just keep glowering. Right now,

Katerina is on her bed, with her legs up leaned against the wall, contemplating her toenails. I, too, am contemplating my toenails, although I am on my bed, with my feet up on my wall, in a kind of mirror image.

This is definitely the most collegiate moment she and I have had together.

"So, why *don't* Russians smile? Seriously."

"What is there to smile for?"

"I dunno. Puppies? Cats playing piano. When a dog becomes friends with a dolphin . . ."

"Endless war, people starving, death—"

"Wow. That went dark fast."

"I am Russian."

"Double depresso."

"You don't understand. You Americans. You think everything is always so great and wonderful and smile all the time."

"Yeah, but do you think we're smiling because we think everything is so great and wonderful or because we want to *make it* great and wonderful?"

"How do I know? I'm not the one acting like puppy dog."

"Look, Americans are optimistic. But is that really so bad? Fact: individuals with the highest levels of optimism have twice the odds of being in ideal cardiovascular health compared to their more pessimistic counterparts."

"So you have healthy heart. You live longer in miserable world."

"Jeez. Okay, what about God? Do you believe in God?"

"Do you believe in Santa Claus?"

"Right. So I'm gonna take that as a no. Okay, so do you think we were all just put on this earth to pay bills and eat sandwiches?"

"Do *you* believe in man with white beard in the sky?"

"Not exactly. But I believe in something. Look, when you do something mean, how do you feel?"

"Not great."

"And when you do something really nice, when nobody even knows about it, how do you feel?"

"Fine. Maybe good."

"Okay, so you have a moral compass. Kind of like an inner guide. Now have you ever stopped to think why you would have that?"

"No."

"Maybe whoever or whatever made us—think of them as our grand programmer—gave that to us. Like, a moral compass!"

"Are you saying we are version of Minecraft?"

"No. But I don't know what we are. Did you know that some of the most preeminent scientific minds, at places like

Princeton and MIT, are coming to the conclusion that this is all a hologram? Our entire lives. A hologram?"

"That is even more depressing."

"No, it's exciting! It means that all this materialism, this conspicuous consumption, this grabbing for money people waste their lives on, is superfluous. And that all that really matters is love and kindness and—"

"You are like human greeting card."

"If I wanted to, believe me, I could curl up into a ball and crawl in the corner and cry for the rest of my life. Considering. But how does that help anything?"

"Don't know."

"Well, at some point I am going to get you to try it out. I'm telling you."

"Try what out?"

"Optimism."

"Disgusting. I will never try."

But she is smiling, there on her side of the room. Both of us contemplating our feet and the possibility that the universe may be a hologram.

"If God is programmer, then who is God's programmer?"

"These are the questions, my dear Katerina, these are the questions . . ."

4

It's a black-and-white photograph on exhibit. Enlarged. Blown up to the size of a painting. In the picture, there's a boy with his face cast upward, a blissful smile on his lips, two shopping packages around his wrist, something wrapped around his head that almost looks like white paper wings. A *Consumer's Dream*. That's the name of the exhibit. The photograph: "In the Sun Next to Detsky Mir Department Store." Moscow. 1961.

We've had to improvise our communication, Madden and me, sans red Beats.

I was told to stand in front of this photograph, at exactly three.

I'm fairly sure someone is supposed to come up beside

me and whisper, *The eagle has landed*. But that's not what happens.

Instead, Madden himself appears. "I thought this particular indictment of conspicuous consumption would appeal to you."

"Wait. What? What are you even doing here?"

"You're not the only one who gets to fly off to exotic locales."

"I just thought there would be some high-tech form of communication here. Not, you know, analog."

"Are you disappointed?"

He smirks.

Hard not to like that smirk.

He hands me a pair of blue Beats.

"Here, better encryption. Still, keep them away from your roommate."

"Ah, just like before. But blue!" I grab them. "Don't be jealous, but I'm going to a rad party. I'd take you but I'm taking your arch nemesis, aka my boyfriend. Of whom you are secretly jealous."

"Hmm. And where exactly is this party?"

"It's my would-be rap-star BFF's birthday. At his dad's . . . DACHA. Boom. Make it rain, bitches!"

"Uri . . . the gangster's son?"

"*Bing bing bing*, you win a gold star."

Madden thinks. And thinks.

"What are you doing? Whatever that is, stop it."

"Actually, that's perfect. That's the perfect place to do it."

"What? Do what?"

"Come on, Paige. You know what."

"Nooooo. C'mon. Really? Can't I just enjoy the party?"

"What are you, five?"

"It's just. Does it have to be there? I mean, can't we, I don't know, stall or whatever? I know I can figure something out."

"We're running out of time. You can do it, or someone less . . . *concerned* can."

"Well, I'm not even going to tell you where the party is, then."

"Paige. You can't take your ball and go home, okay? We're way past that. You know it and I know it. Listen. I'll have a gun planted."

"But I hate guns. No gu—"

"Please await further instructions."

He strolls away. "By the way, don't miss the third-floor exhibit. Huge vaginas. Very provocative."

"They're probably giant vagina dentatas because all men fear the power of the female!" I'm basically yelling this across an empty room. Madden ignores me.

The security guard only raises an eyebrow.

5

This is it. The last video. I can't wait to tell you how I got these.

But not yet.

From above we are looking at it. The gold-and-robin's-egg-blue gilded Baroque restaurant. Underling has just come in, excited. He whispers something into Dimitri's ear.

Queen Elsa picks at her blinchiki with a fork.

Dimitri turns to her.

"Get packed. We are going to Dubai."

"I thought we were going to America?"

"No. Better deal. From sultan."

"But I want to go to America. Girl have better life there.

I will be next Hillary Clinton. Or maybe even Kim Kardashian!"

"Ha! Dream on, *mishka*. We go to Dubai. That is good place to be billionaire. If you don't like it you can go back to cabbage farm."

Underling leaves.

Queen Elsa frowns at her plate.

"Don't worry. You will like. We will have yacht. Palace. Gold. Don't frown, *mishka*. You will be number one girl in my harem."

He winks and raises his glass.

"*Dosvedanya.*"

6

Ice-skating in Red Square looks a little bit like ice-skating in Disneyland minus the big brother element. Actually, now that I think about it, they're not that different.

Above us, the GUM Department Store (aka Glavny Universalny Magazin), is lit up in white Christmas lights, serving as a kind of princess fantasy backdrop to this ice-skating wonderland.

Raynes and I have swerved off the main rink into this white-and-red tent where it's extremely quainty. Hot chocolate. Spiked hot chocolate. Glogg. Gluehwein. And lots of other hot alcoholic drinks that start with *GL*.

We're both laughing at ourselves because we're the worst ice skaters to ever ice-skate the face of the earth. Particularly here. It's a good thing everyone else is so drunk, because otherwise we would probably have been kicked out of the rink. I'm sure everyone assumed we were five sheets to the wind.

It's clear that most of these people are not just drunk but Russian drunk. Which means their bodies are moving forward and they're totally cogent but every once in a while they just randomly tip over.

Raynes sits down at a corner table, underneath a string of white Christmas lights. And yes, Oleg is behind us. Brooding.

He was not ice-skating.

Of course he was not ice-skating.

"God, I'm so bad at this." Raynes laughs, taking off his skates.

"Me too. What were we thinking?" I'm taking off mine, too. I guess that ends that microhumiliation. "I mean, I suppose we were going for the sort of romance of it."

We lock eyes. I think we're both maybe thinking that we didn't need ice-skating to be romantic. At least that's what I'm thinking. Also, I have to kill you in a few days. And think of a way *not* to have to kill you.

"Do you think we can get Oleg to fetch us some hot chocolate?"

"Oh, I'm sure he's dying to. He's coming with us to the

dacha party, of course. Sorry. I can't seem to get him to take the night off."

I don't say, *Oh, that complicates my plan to kill you.* Instead, I smile and say, "Well, we knew he was coming, right?"

"Oh, he's coming all right. I think the whole thing makes him nervous."

"Do you think he's paranoid?" Deflection, ladies and gentlemen!

Raynes shrugs. "Who knows?"

"I mean, there's really no reason to guard you. It's not like you're doing anything that would make anyone dislike you." This is my not-so-subtle way of trying to get him to admit his diabolical plan to expose RAITH.

"I think the American government, and probably half the country, would beg to differ."

And he leans in to kiss me. Right here, under the white sparkly Christmas lights in the Red Square ice rink.

FLASH!

What I can only imagine to be a Russian paparazzo snaps a picture. He smiles for a tenth of a second before Oleg bowls him over and pins him to the ground.

Now everyone starts to look over at us. Some people are taking pictures on their phones. I have a millisecond thought that maybe somehow Gael García Bernal will see one of these pictures someday.

"Guess it's time to smile for the cameras." I shrug.

Raynes smiles. "At least they didn't get us while we were ice-skating."

And in that moment, this moment here, I try not to fall in love with him. And I wonder, in these pictures that these people are taking, if it will show. Here is a picture of a girl about to murder her boyfriend.

7

This will probably be my last jaunt along the Moskva River. Not only because I'm starting to freeze to death, but also because my mission is soon to be accomplished. One way or the other.

Madden's voice comes over my blue Beats, and I just know this is going to be annoying.

"Paige, they found out."

"Who?"

"FSB. They figured it out. They know about the flash drive."

"Oh Jesus."

"It's not good. They have a plan."

"Are you going to tell me that plan or are you just going to say dramatically, 'They have a plan'?"

"They're planning on taking Raynes. From the dacha. They're going to kidnap him and pin it on Dimitri. They'll tell everyone he's dead. The great Raynes is dead. Then, my guess is they'll probably shoot Dimitri. Two birds with one stone."

"Do you know where they're planning on taking him?"

"Yes, Paige. They're planning on taking him to McDonald's. Then Disneyland. *Or a secret jail where we'll never be able to find him.* And they'll torture him. Until he gives up the list. And all our RAITH agents die."

"Okay, I get it."

"Paige, he can't be caught alive. Now that the flash drive is gone, now that there's no backup, they can do whatever they want with him. If he's dead, no loss. But they won't just kill him. They'll get the list out of him. They'll torture him. You're doing him a favor. To kill him first. Do you understand that?"

"Yes. Un-fucking-fortunately."

"It's the right thing to do."

"Isn't that what they always say?"

The sun is setting behind Kadashi Church, taking any thought of the heat with it. Now it's freezing and I can see my breath.

I've never been so cold.

8

There's a moment, a moment where I'm sitting on the foot of the bed waiting for Raynes. I'm all gussied up for the big party. And there he is, stepping out of the shower. And I wish I could just stop this train and get off.

He's telling me about a dream he had last night.

"So, I'm falling, falling off a high building and it's terrifying and I'm just flailing around, trying to scream but nothing's coming out. And right before the bottom, right before I'm just about to hit the sidewalk and splatter into a million pieces, you suddenly appear . . . and you lift me. Gently, smiling, up even higher than the building, higher than the skyline . . . up, up, up into the clouds. And I'm so grateful. In my dream, I'm so grateful to you."

Gulp.

I smile back at him, feigning a kind of sweet under-standing.

Oh God. I can't live with myself.

He's telling me about a sweet dream he had where I'm, like, an angel or superhero, and in reality I'm just about to lead him to his death.

I'm going to hell. If there's a hell. This is my entry ticket.

"You know . . . we don't have to go to this party. Maybe we could just stay here and watch Netflix or something? I really have to catch up on my binge-watching."

"What? No. Are you crazy? Oleg is *letting me go* to this. I can't miss it!"

Netflix. It was a pathetic attempt. A last-minute Hail Mary. And I didn't sell it.

"You look really beautiful tonight, Paige. I'll have to have Oleg fend off all your adoring would-be suitors."

Oleg, who is standing by the front door, pretends not to hear.

If Madden is right, he's probably too focused on his plan to kidnap Raynes later tonight at the dacha.

He catches me staring at him. Maybe he heard my

thought. Maybe he feels guilty. The two of us stare at each other for a second, taking the other one in. Then he looks away.

Maybe he can tell I feel guilty, too.

9

Sometimes Russians have a modest little dacha maybe a few hours outside of Moscow, a little wooden cabin with firewood and a stove. In winter, even the mice freeze to death.

That is not this dacha.

Or try it like this:

THIS. DACHA.

All caps.

This estate, one hour outside of Moscow, makes just about everything in the States look like a strip mall. It's a three-story stone palace, bright royal blue, with an elaborate white stone crest-type thing at the top, amid the spires. The entire face is covered with elaborate white engravings and moldings and etchings all around the doors and the windows and everything else you can imagine. There are little circles and spires and playful touches in the façade, as well as white stripes on the first floor. It sounds completely bizarro, I know, but it's truly one of the most beautiful things I've ever seen. I actually gasp when we turn through the forest to see it.

"Holy smokes."

I guess Raynes feels the same way, too. "Wow."

He grabs my hand as if to say, *Isn't it cool that we're here, together, in this beautiful place? You and me?*

I hold his hand but want to jump out into the snow and become a snowman.

We drive down a long, tree-lined driveway to the dacha, lit up for the party. Even through the windows, you can hear the music practically shaking the snow off the ground. Missy Elliott. "WTF (Where They From)."

Sidebar: I love Missy Elliott.

I feel like she's the queen of everything.

"What do you think? Are we fashionably late?" Raynes quips.

"I think we are perfectly late. Looks like they're really going for it, doesn't it?"

"Do you think the toilets inside are gold?"

"I don't know, but if the inside looks anything like the outside, I think I'm never leaving. You might have to drag me out."

(Or I'll drag *you* out, because you'll be dead.)

Oleg walks behind us as we make our grand entrance. Although it's not much of an entrance because everyone is too busy having the time of their life. Seriously, these Russians are not fooling around. No droll looks and rolling of eyes around here. These people are really going for it. Partying like the world is ending.

Across the throngs of arms in the air, lights, confetti, and lithe lady acrobats on giant thin crimson velvet curtains doing gravity-defying tricks, there is Uri. He is, of course, in full hip-hop attire and surrounded by adoring throngs.

"Ah, there he is."

I take Raynes by the hand, leading him to Uri, hoping to lose Oleg in the bacchanalian masses. I don't see Katerina, but that's a good thing. Between Oleg and Katerina, Raynes could be nabbed at any time. I have to keep him close. I have to keep him in full view of everyone.

Until I don't.

Until I kill him.

(Until I can find some way out of killing him.)

(Look, I don't know what I'm doing, okay? The jury is still behind closed doors, and that door is locked. Everyone can just stand outside waiting.)

Uri sees us and yells over the music.

"My friends! You see! Little party for birthday!"

"Yes. I see! Very little party! Uri, this is Sean Raynes; Sean Raynes, this is Uri. This modest little soiree is to celebrate his birth. In case you were confused, although he is not actually Jesus Christ."

"No, I am rap star! Well, not yet. But someday . . ."

"You want a drink?" Raynes is about to walk off to the bar.

"No, wait! I'll go with you!"

"It's okay, you can stay here and talk to the birthday boy."

"No, no, no. I have very elaborate drink tastes. Very specific. It'd be way too complicated to explain, so—"

Raynes is staring at me. He's thinking that I'm acting weird because I *am* acting weird. I really need to work on duplicity. I am horrendous at it.

We part with Uri and head for the bar.

Just in time to see Katerina.

Okay, looks like I don't have much time. I better speed it up. Before Oleg or Katerina kidnaps him and ships him to Siberia, or the gulag, or wherever it is the FSB ships people off to so they can do illegal, invisible torture to them.

God I don't want to do this God I don't want to do this God I don't want to do this.

"You know, do you think we could get some air? It's kind

of insane in here. I think I'm getting claustrophobic."

"Sure. You don't want to get an elaborate drink that's too complicated for me to remember, first?"

"No, I definitely need to get some air. It's, like, a physical reaction I have to enclosed spaces swarming with people. Also, I think I might be allergic to the confetti."

Raynes raises an eyebrow.

"All right."

We are just about to make it out the back door. The idea is that the gun is strategically placed under this picturesque white outdoor gazebo in the snow. I'm supposed to lead Raynes over there, casually drop something, grab the gun, and shoot my boyfriend.

Simple, right?

I can feel my chest tightening and the air, much thinner up here, not wanting to have anything to do with me. Just breathe, Paige. Try not to get ahead of yourself.

We come out the back, the cold air whooshing in past us, and I see the white gazebo. A fairy-tale picture in the snow.

"Oh, how cool! Look at that gazebo!"

This is my oh-so-not-subtle way of steering him over there.

Except.

He doesn't reply. I guess he doesn't like gazebos. Or cold. Or snow. Or murder attempts. Or else maybe he didn't hear me. Or else maybe he didn't hear me because he's not behind me.

Oh.

Right.

Yeah.

He's not behind me.

In fact, he's not anywhere to be seen.

10

"Paige!"

It's coming from down below, from what I'm assuming is the servant's quarters, or the maid's quarters, or the serf's quarters, or whatever passage it is the oppressed people use to go in and out.

There's a stone walkway leading down to the cellar, and the footsteps echo out from there.

Using the magic of my phone, I shine a light down the cellar, where there seems to be some kind of underground passageway. It's actually pretty gross in here, but I'm choosing not to focus on that right now. Also, sidebar, phones make really good flashlights, but the reverse is not true.

There he is. Oleg, of course, dragging a half-conscious

Raynes out with him. I guess he must have clocked him after he yelled out to me. Bastard!

I'm gonna get this guy.

Here in the shadows . . . he kind of looks like Ted Cruz. And honestly, that just makes my job that much easier.

As is my habit, I start seeing myself from above again or, in this case, the musty stone ceiling above us. It's okay, I think you're probably getting used to it by now.

I watch myself take a running start to tackle him, and that works pretty well, until he flips me over. He used my momentum against me. I should've known better, honestly. That's like Karate 101. My dojo master would be shaking his head.

Raynes uses the opportunity, even in his half daze, to shove Oleg into the wall.

Thank God. This gives me an opportunity to get up and, somehow, energized by the incredible pain just bestowed upon my back, unleash everything I learned on the Muay Thai mat, right there in front of Raynes. Who had no idea. He probably thought I was some kind of shrinking violet.

I guess they don't teach the art of the eight limbs at FSB. Or, if they do, Oleg is rusty. It's a sort of sequence of moves. Counter Oleg's right cross with a Thai jab coming over his punch. Counter a left hook with a cover and follow with the left elbow. Roundhouse kick. At this point Oleg is supremely annoyed. I try to finish off this whole escapade with a reverse roundhouse kick, but Oleg doesn't like being beat up by a girl, so he summons every last bit of his strength to throw me against the wall.

And that works.

So now there are Tweety Birds again, but it doesn't matter.

I'm getting to know these Tweety Birds pretty well lately.

Never fear, *mon ami*. Yes, Oleg has brute strength, but I have the art of the eight limbs.

So, a new sequence: right elbow, step-up knee strike, roundhouse kick, and, finally, a cobra punch . . . otherwise known as a superman punch. These are all not nice things to do to anyone. Even your worst enemy. But I guess Oleg is applying for the job.

And he isn't happy right now.

And by "isn't happy right now" I mean "is on the ground, whimpering."

See. Here's the thing. He's extremely strong. There is no doubt. And he did manage to land a couple of blows that are going to take some ice and make me look like a street urchin for the next three weeks. I know that.

But I think I studied harder at my dojo.

You see, practice makes perfect.

And now we know. Oleg isn't as tough as we thought.

That really is a lesson, isn't it? Just because someone has

a black leather jacket and a mean scowl does not mean that they are the Terminator.

Honestly, he's three times slower than Katerina. Who, praise the Lord and pass the cornflakes, is nowhere to be found.

Then I would *really* be in trouble. I definitely could not take Oleg and Katerina at the same time. I'm nowhere near that good.

"Paige?! Where did you—"

"C'mon. This way. We don't have much time."

I grab him and lead him out, back into the snow. Back next to, yes, the fateful white gazebo.

"Um, where did you learn how to fight like that?"

But now I'm crouched down, looking for the planted gun.

Sidebar: I really wish they would have given me anything but a gun. A poison dart maybe. A laser blaster. A lightsaber. *Anything.*

But no. Had to be a dumb, annoying, phallic, stupid, loser gun.

"Can I ask you a question?" This is it; my last chance for an out. "If you had to do something on principle, but people could maybe die, *would* probably die . . . would you do it?"

"I guess it depends on the principle." He shrugs.

Still looking for the gun. Still looking for an out.

"Well, what if you *knew* people would die, but it was a really important principle?"

"Yes. I would."

Fuck.

Well, there goes that chance.

Ah! And there is the gun. Right on time.

"Why are you asking?"

But now I'm up, pointing the gun at him. "Because I've been hiding something from you."

"Jesus! Paige! What the fuck?!"

"Why the hell would you ever release that list? Seriously. Why the hell do you have to do something so destructive? So heartless?"

"What list?"

"Don't play dumb. I know all about it. The list. The RAITH operatives."

"Paige, RAITH is illegal. It is an illegal, unconstitutional spy agency that is beholden to no one. It has to be exposed. You know what the fall of the Roman Empire looked like? Secrets. Secret trials. People taken away in the middle of the night for no reason. With no trial. No due process. Paranoia. Suspicion. Fearmongering. Sound familiar?"

"People will die. Horrible deaths."

"Isn't that the price of liberty?"

"Liberty? At what point does liberty become your folly?

Your vanity project? Your attempt at fame, or maintaining your fame? Are you sure this isn't some narcissistic attempt to solidify yourself in the international canon? Have you really thought about this? Not romantically. But with your fucking soul? Because I know you, or I *thought* I knew you. And this? This kind of blind disregard for human life? For the people left behind? For their children? It's not you. It's not the you I know. It's not the you I fell in love with."

Raynes is looking at me, and that last part . . . that last couple of sentences . . . I feel like I got through. Maybe.

We stand there, our breath in puffs in the freezing air.

"Look, I think I can save you. But you can't release the list."

"You know it will be released if you kill me. You know there's a backup."

"Sorry. There's no backup."

"Yeah, right."

"The flash drive? I figured it out."

"Sure."

"Monument Valley."

The expression on his face changes. I wouldn't think he could have gotten any paler, but somehow it's possible.

"Paige. What have you done?"

"I've saved people's fucking lives is what I've done! And I can save your life, too. If you come with me, I can get you out of this goddamned country, because you're dead here. You're dead practically everywhere. Your only hope is to come home. I can get you home. But you can't release the list."

"Paige, I'll go to jail at home. I'll spend the rest of my life looking at a fucking concrete wall. You know that."

"Would you literally rather die? Because they're gonna kill you here! They're gonna torture you, they're gonna get the list, and anything else you might have, and kill you. Oleg. The FSB. They're gonna make it look like you died here. Tonight. And you're never gonna see the light of day again. And you're gonna wish you were dead. Look. Just tell me you're not gonna release the list and I'll figure it out. I won't have to kill you."

We share a moment. The gun still trained on him. The snow beginning to fall in pristine, gentle snowflakes that have nothing to do with killing or death or worldwide conspiracies.

"I can save you, Raynes. Just give me a chance."

"I can't do it, Paige. I'm sorry."

"Not as sorry as me."

I raise the gun and take a deep breath.

"You better make peace with whatever you have to make peace with."

It might look to some people like there's something, some

water welling up in the sides of my eyes. But I'm tough. I can do this. All I have to do is think of my mother. Think of my father. My family. Our little sweet family that gives to charity and shops at the organic market together and packs Christmas boxes for the homeless in December. All I have to do is think about our little family and how I want that little family back, along with kindness and organic soap and random paintings my mom buys from street artists while my dad shakes his head.

And now I'm crying. My entire face is covered in tears and it's freezing and all I want is my family back, my life back and not to be here in the middle of this bone-chilling Russian night with a gun pointed at someone who I wasn't supposed to fall in love with but kind of fell in love with.

He looks back up at me. An almost imperceptible nod.

This is it.

"I'm sorry. I'm so fucking sorry."

I say it through tears.

BANG.

The shot comes faster than I thought. It rings out through the trees. But it's not Raynes that drops.

It's me.

11

The shot hits me square in the chest and lands me on the ground, snow two feet all around me.

Raynes looks down in shock and then sees Oleg, hobbling across the snow, heading toward him.

"RUN!"

"But I can't just leave you here—"

"Fucking run!"

And Raynes takes off into the trees. It's nice to know he was a gentleman about that. Very polite.

I know you're wondering if I'm dead now. If this whole thing has been a posthumous monologue from beyond the grave. Please don't cry. I'm fine. No, really. Madden wouldn't let me go to the party without a bulletproof vest. I tried to talk him out of it because it wasn't very flattering. Let's just be honest, something like that is hard to carry off. But he insisted. And now I'm glad he insisted. It's just annoying that I'm going to have to tell him he was right.

Welp, I could lie here making snow angels all day, except Raynes is being pursued into the forest by Oleg, who basically looks like a lumbering zombie in a leather jacket.

I get to see all this from my view in the snow, so it's kind of sideways. A snow half frame and then a half-turned forest with Raynes running one way and Oleg running after him, shooting.

I have to get up any time now, and I keep telling my body to do just that, but my body isn't listening. My chest is pounding and it felt like, you know what it felt like? It felt like someone hit me as hard as they could in the chest with a hammer. So I'll just watch here from my leisurely sideways recline in the snow.

The problem is that Oleg, despite his uneven footing, seems to be gaining on poor ol' Raynes. That's the thing about these computer geniuses. You get the feeling they all got an F in gym.

Before I know it, two new figures enter my tilted frame, and just like that, one of those figures takes aim and shoots—at Oleg. Who falls to the ground. And stays there. I'm not sure if he got issued a bulletproof vest from FSB. It doesn't really look like it. But I'll keep an eye on him.

One of these men is old and bald, walking slower. The other, in hot pursuit, is the one who shot Oleg. You know who it is, right?

Yup. You guessed it.

Uri's mobbed-up father, Dimitri, and his favorite side-kick, Underling.

Underling is a lot faster than anyone so far in this here relay, and he catches up to Raynes quickly, tackles him, and then that's that.

So now the mobsters have Raynes.

Jesus.

My body finally decides to acquiesce, and I get up slowly. I'm dusting myself off, about to run after Raynes and his two new best friends, when something whooshes past me on the right.

"What the—?"

Oh, great. There's Katerina on a snowmobile flying across the snow toward the lot of them.

That's right. How could I forget? FSB wants Raynes dead. Katerina works for FSB. Katerina is after Raynes, too. To kill him. Before he leaves Russia.

Check.

I guess Christmas Eve is officially over.

"Are you serious right now?"

I look up to the heavens above, but no answer.

12

My sorry self is hobbling across the snow just in time to see Underling point and shoot.

BLAM!

Katerina's snowmobile takes a hit, sending her flying to the ground. She rolls off into the snowdrift.

Now Dimitri and Underling are free to steal Raynes with abandon.

I hobble-run over to Katerina, who lies there recovering in the snow.

"Are you okay?"

"Yes, wonderful."

"Well, you don't have to be sarcastic."

"Yes, I do. I was born this way."

"Okay, well, I think you should just stay here now, okay? You might be hurt."

"Yes, of course."

She immediately kicks me off my feet and goes running after Raynes, Dimitri, and Underling.

"You bitch! That really was not very nice."

Katerina is running off into the snow. "*Nice* is for talk show and day care."

I get up and start running after her.

"Well, I'm gonna have to shoot you now! So that's basically karma!"

We're yelling at each other over the snow.

"You won't shoot."

"I have dissociative disorder, you know!"

"I thought you hate gun."

"I do. That's why I don't want to shoot!"

"Nice try."

She keeps running away through the snow. Of course, she's a much faster runner than me. Part of her bionic Russian training.

"Katerina, stop! Or I'll shoot!"

"Then fucking shoot!"

"Okay, I'm gonna shoot you in the ankle, okay? They say that's the safest place."

"Don't shoot me, just go home."

"I can't! Okay, I'm gonna shoot you now, and then when I do, just stay down, okay?"

"Why are you so weird?! If you are going to shoot, then fucking shoot!"

"O-kay! Are you ready?!"

"What is wrong with you?!"

BANG.

She goes down.

I run up to her, bleeding out the side of her calf.

"Oh, I meant to hit a little lower, actually."

She gets up. I think she actually believes she's going to catch up with these guys. Gunshot and all.

I kick her in the chest.

"This is interesting friendship."

"Stay. The hell. Down. You're bleeding pretty bad, honestly. It really behooves you to stay down."

Katerina, the wind knocked out of her, looks down at her bleeding leg. There's no way she can keep up.

"Look. You tried. You gave it your best shot. And that's really what counts."

"Do I get participation trophy?"

Just then, another snowmobile comes flying past.

It's Uri.

"Jesus Christ. What the fuck is happening right now? Look, you'll be okay. You have about two hours to get inside before you freeze to death. You should be able to make it."

She looks up at me, and a funny little smile takes over the side of her mouth.

"I think positive."

I smile and it hits me that after this mission, whatever happens, I may never see Katerina again.

"Come see me in the horrible imperialist United States."

"I will, puppy dog. I bring vodka."

We share a look of acknowledgment. So this is friendship. The sad part. The part you avoid by not letting anyone in in the first place.

I give her a smile before taking off after Uri and everybody else who seems to be coming out of the woodwork.

"You're an alcoholic!" I yell it over my shoulder.

Not sure if she hears me over Uri's snowmobile.

13

Quite frankly, by the time I get to the clearing there's a lot to process.

First, there's a clearing in the forest. Check. Second, there's a small runway, the type usually used for a prop plane. Check. Third, there's a private jet, there in the middle of the winter wonderland. Check. Fourth, I can't see Raynes any-where, but I am assuming he's on the plane as he seems to be the crown jewel of this whole enterprise.

But wait, there's more!

Standing on the steps coming out of the plane is Ice Queen. Sidebar: I really like her outfit. She's wearing a kind of faux-fur hat thing, so she kind of resembles a Russian Q-tip. But she's making it work. I understand that fashion is probably the last thing I should be thinking about, but it's important to stop and smell the roses.

Now Uri is standing there, having ditched his snowmobile in a snowbank and also having what appears to be an extremely passionate conversation with his dad, Dimitri. When I was little, my dad used to read me Roald Dahl stories at night before bed: *Charlie and the Chocolate Factory*, *The Twits*, *James and the Giant Peach* . . . You get the picture. I am fairly certain Dimitri never read books to Uri at bedtime.

This suspicion is confirmed when Dimitri nods at Queen Elsa and she raises her gun at Uri.

Yes, let's think about that for a second. Dimitri, Uri's own father, just gave the order to kill his own son.

Nice guy.

I am not a fan of Uri's rap stylings, but I think it's rude to kill your own son. So I raise my gun—effing gun, I hate you—one more time and aim at Ice Queen. Sorry, darling, at least you'll be caught dead in an extremely chic getup.

Sayonara, Ice Queen.

BLAM!

Wait.

That wasn't me.

I didn't even fire yet.

And that's not Uri on the ground either. No, folks. Uri is standing right there. Happy as a clam.

Can you guess who's on the ground?

Yep, you guessed it.

Dimitri.

Moscow kingpin and generally satanic guy is writhing around in the snow. At least he's alive to look up and see his son kiss his girlfriend.

"Wait. What the hell?"

I say it, mostly to the tree I'm hiding behind. But I'm sure Dimitri is thinking it, too.

This is a really long kiss. I mean, it's still happening.

And still happening.

Annnnd still happening.

"Jesus, get a room."

But the tree doesn't laugh.

And before I know it, Uri and Queen Elsa are stepping onto the plane, leaving Dimitri to roll around in the snow and feel like a damned fool. Through one of the windows, I can make out Raynes near the back. Yup. They got him.

"Wait! Wait wait wait wait!"

I take off after them.

But they can't hear me over the engine. I'm running through the snow toward them, but now the wind is picking up.

The plane is getting ready for takeoff, with its engine

blasting and the snow whipping around in a frenzy, and this is basically it.

This is it.

The plane is literally leaving the runway, and I blew it.

I fucking blew it.

14

I never was that good at being brave.

Even the small things I did, the jujitsu, the fancy stuff, I always knew I would win. Against those lunkheads in the Applebee's? Against those lunkheads in the alley behind the bunker bar? I knew I would win. And it's not truly brave if you know you're going to win.

But this . . .

This I can't win.

This is an airplane, taking off, on a snowy runway somewhere outside of Moscow. Who am I, Ethan Hunt? On my best days, I'd be sunk. But now, hobbling around in the snow after being shot and kicked and then kicked again. Forget it. That's all she wrote.

Somewhere to my left, through the snow, I can hear Dimitri rolling around, swearing to himself.

"You're a horrible father!"

I yell it over the engine.

"And you are weak American. Go home to Mommy."

He practically spits it out at me.

And that's when it hits me. This is it for home. This is it for my family. For my mom and my dad and whatever life, whatever future, we have together.

No.

No, I won't go quietly into the night.

Before I know it I am running with everything I have to the end of the tarmac to beat the airplane. I get about thirty feet from the tip of the nose, right there, right in front of it in the runway, blocking its path.

It's just me, now, little beat-up me with the snow swirling all around in circles and the sound of the jet engine like a shriek. It's just me against this plane.

What is it Viva said in training? Before I crashed the Viper? If you lose control on a wet or snowy surface, it can be much harder to regain control.

I have to get closer.

The closer I get, the more they're forced to jerk to the side.

And lose control.

On a wet or snowy surface.

(In this case, practically an ice-skating rink.)

I get closer.

And closer still.

I stand there, looking up into the cockpit, right at the pilot. I stand there. One small girl against the world.

And it's not me looking at me from above anymore. Suddenly, it's me inside myself, not from a distance. Suddenly, I get to be me again.

There's no irony to it, no snark, no safety belts, no precautions.

In this moment, this moment where I get to be me again, I stand for everything that I've ever known and everything that I've ever loved.

And I stand tall.

Later, I get to hear the recap of the conversation in the cockpit at this very moment. It goes something like this . . .

Pilot: "You want I run her over? She is already injured, so it wouldn't be—"

Uri: "No! No. Just give me a second . . . FUCK! These American girls are so annoying!"

And then he gives the order.

But what it looks like from here, from down here on the tarmac . . .

Is that I stopped the plane.

I stopped.

A.

Goddamned.

Airplane.

15

I've never been on a private jet before. All I can really gather, in my cursory inspection of the cabin, is that I guess billionaires really like wood paneling. That's fine. I'm not here to judge. But I will tell you this. You could shoot an American Apparel ad in here, against any of these walls, without paying a cent on production design. And I'm pretty sure that's not what they were going for.

Raynes is sitting in the back, handcuffed to his seat.

"Is that really necessary? I mean, what's he going to do? Fly out at ten thousand feet? Make a hot move out into the abyss?"

"It is precaution."

That's Ice Queen.

"Okay, I just have to tell you that you're basically slaying it with that hat."

She looks genuinely surprised.

"But please tell me that's not real fur."

"No. It's Valentino."

"Oh, I love Valentino! I really liked his fall collection last year. I especially liked that dress with the heart on it. The chiffon one."

Uri looks at the two of us, puzzled.

"Yes. I have dress." Wow. Queen Elsa actually possesses the bee's knees of all dresses made in the history of mankind.

"Okay, I'm totally peanut butter and jealous."

She smiles.

See.

Social skills.

"Uri, I would just like to thank you for not running me over."

"You are welcome, but you are also pain in my asshole."

"Right. I get it. But, Uri, I think it behooves me to ask . . . what in the actual hell is going on here? You do realize your dad is, like, rolling around on the tarmac back there in the snow."

And this is true. I can only imagine him cursing the heavens above as we ascended into the great wide open.

Karma.

"You see, American Paige, your boyfriend is expensive man. He catch good price. My father wanted to sell him to highest bidder. In this case, highest bidder was sultan in Dubai."

"So we're going to Dubai?"

"Not quite." Queen Elsa is very pleased with herself.

"You see, I have girlfriend, too." Uri gives a loving look to Queen Elsa, who, I have to admit, is not so Ice-y anymore.

"And girlfriend tells me secret. And I get better deal. Citizenship. In America. And price. Not as big. But America is place for hip-hop. Is worth it."

"Wait. From who? From the CIA?"

"No. From horrible Republican billionaire who want to parade him around like pink pony. Maybe tip next election."

"Maybe make pageant for hillbilly."

That's Ice Queen. She doesn't seem to like hillbilly.

"So, where are we landing?"

"Texas."

"NOOOOOOOOOOooooooooooooo! No no no no no! Okay, listen to me. Raynes? Are you listening?"

"Um. Yes."

"You're going to go to jail. You know that, right?"

"Pretty much."

"You're going to rot inside a jail for the rest of your life. No reporters. No soapbox. Nothing. Forever. Like, even after the singularity. Like, I'll be half robot and you will still be an inferior full human. And our cyborg/human forbidden love will be prohibited yet romantic."

Queen Elsa and Uri share a look.

"But that's not important right now! What's important is . . . I can fix this. If . . . you promise . . . you *promise* not to release the list. I'm not saving you just for you to let all those other people die. No way. Do you understand?"

Raynes looks at me.

"So, to recap: your choices are . . . rot in jail past the singularity, which is speculated to be around two thousand forty-three, or . . . destroy the list and I'll save you."

Uri chimes in.

"Sounds like easy choice, bro."

"Don't say *bro*." That's me.

"Why not? Why not say *bro*?"

"Sound like douche bag." That's Ice Queen.

She and I share a look. The international language of girl-dom.

Raynes thinks it over. We stare at each other in a temporary détente.

"Were you really going to kill me back there?"

"I'm pretty sure I wasn't going to. But I'm not one hundred percent sure. I'm like ninety-eight percent sure. Maybe ninety-seven."

"What stopped you?"

"Well, duh. I kind of like you. A little bit. Not like a lot. Like *oh, I think about this person at night and I wonder what they're doing and when I listen to Elliott Smith it makes me think of him because we listened to him at Ramallah Café one night high above the Moscow city lights . . .*"

"How romantic." That moment of sarcasm was brought to you by Ice Queen.

Raynes and I share a look. Finally, he nods.

"Okay."

"Do I have your word?"

"Yes. You have my word."

"YAAAASSS!!" I jump about three feet in the air. "Also, I would like to offer you the side opportunity of being my boyfriend."

He smiles. "I don't think so."

"Ouch." Uri chimes in.

"It's okay. I get it. I know we might have some trust issues. It's hard to get over it when your girlfriend almost kills you."

Raynes and I share a look. We're okay. Whatever happens, he and I, we're Switzerland.

I turn to Uri. "Okay, now, Uri. Do you really want to be an American?"

"Of course. I going to be hip-hop star."

Again, Queen Elsa and I share a look. I think we have both decided to spare him the conversation about unrealistic expectations. "Okay, well, here's the thing, Uri. I'm going to ask you, now, to do something. And I'm going to tell you what I know to be true, in my heart of hearts, way underneath all my snarkiness and sarcasm. But the truth is . . . being an American doesn't have to do with having a fast car or a lot of money or being famous. It means doing the right thing. And I'm asking you now, Uri. I'm asking you with all my heart, here, to do the right thing."

"*Da.*" Uri puffs his narrow chest. "I will be best American."

"Excellent. Where's your phone?"

16

The arrival terminal of the Oakland International Airport is white and stainless steel, with a sign above the entry that says "Welcome!" in over forty different languages: "*Dobrodošli,* 欢迎, *Vítáme tě, Bienvenue,* ابحرم, *Willkommen, Καλώς, Aloha, Benvenuto, Shalom, Dobro pozhalovat.*"

It's a sleepy airport. Usually fairly empty.

Except today.

Today, the Oakland International Airport looks almost like Coachella.

The entire entry is covered from wall to wall with a sea of expectant faces, signs, and banners.

Let's be honest. Most of them are Berkeley students and faculty. But there's quite a few people from San Francisco, too, and Portland, and eight news trucks parked outside with journalists rushing all over the place and, yes, even some celebrities. I don't mean to drop names, but there is Susan Sarandon and Mark Ruffalo, and over there is Michael Moore. Don't look over. Just act casual. Stop it, you're embarrassing me.

If you're wondering if they're here to see you, I'm sorry to burst your bubble, but the answer is no. And they're certainly not here to see me, as I am just a cog in the proverbial wheel.

But this cog in the wheel did manage to do something I never thought this cog in the wheel could do.

This cog managed . . . through God or Buddha or Allah or Yahweh or whoever you happen to believe in . . . to sound the alarm through Twitter, Facebook, Tumblr, Instagram, Snapchat, email, smoke signals, messenger pigeon, and anything else you can imagine.

I told them Raynes was coming.

I told them where we were landing.

And when.

And I told them, everyone, that they had to come, and bring everyone they knew or had ever met who cared about this country and the future of this country.

I told them Sean Raynes would be taken to some super-secret prison under the cover of night and probably executed unless they were there. All of them.

That they were his last shot at freedom.

And that this was their moment.

You want to know a secret? Something I wouldn't tell a soul except for you, who I'm telling now, now that we've been through so much together? I really didn't think this was going to work. I thought I was crazy. I thought I was grasping at straws. I thought *I* might go to jail.

But looking out at the hundreds and hundreds of faces, all cheering Raynes, throngs of them, forming a circle around Raynes, protecting Raynes, chanting, "Liberty!" and, "Our rights! Raynes rights!" it hits me. It's actually working.

The police are just standing there, on the outskirts of the throngs, looking at one another, waiting for an order. But there's no order being given. Even if they could get to him, no one wants to be the one to give the order; no one wants to drag Raynes out in front of the cameras. Not with all of this. It could be a career ender. For the police. For the mayor. For whoever it is that gives that order.

And I could kiss this Northern California liberal ground.

Because it worked.

No one had to die in the end.

Mission accomplished.

17

There's a dark brown wooden trellis above us, covered in bright fuchsia bougainvillea. Below it, staring at me from above my almond milk latte, is Madden.

"You'll be happy to know your best friend Uri was granted asylum, along with his extremely attractive girlfriend. And given a handsome sum. As a goodwill gesture."

"She really is crazily pretty, isn't she? It's almost like she's an alien or something. I call her Ice Queen."

"That's apt."

Over the speakers, George Ezra is singing *Budapest*. It's a happy, soulful little song, and it seems like all of our troubles have somehow floated away beyond the hot pink bougainvillea.

"So, dearest Madden, on a scale of one to ten . . . am I fired?"

"What, for completely disobeying orders and bringing public enemy number one back to the center of the liberal universe so we would have to actually pardon him?"

"Something like that."

"You know, this may surprise you, but the president of the United States, *your* commander in chief, wanted me to express her gratitude. She said she admires your moxie."

"Wow. The president of the United States admires my moxie. Are you jealous?"

"Maybe. It's possible. No one has ever said anything about *my* moxie."

I slurp through my smirk.

"By the way, I have some interesting videotapes to show you. If you care. Of Uri's dad. Dimitri. We planted a camera at Turandot. His favorite restaurant. You're even in one of the videos. Looking quite clueless, I'm afraid."

"Ah! Looking forward to it."

See, it was Madden all along. With the videotapes. Now you can sleep at night.

You're welcome.

"So? What about my parents? I think I've proven myself. Don't you?"

"You have. And we know where they are. Now we just have to get to them."

"Now *I* just have to get to them."

"You think you're ready for that?"

I stare at him. Duh.

"You'll have to learn Arabic."

"I'll start tonight."

"That's what I thought. You're a tough cookie. I respect that. Even if you are annoying."

We smile at each other. It's almost like seeing an old friend. Someone from long, long ago.

"And Raynes?"

He shrugs. "Look, he's got the best legal team in the country. Paid for by everyone from MoveOn to Sean Penn.

"Yeah, I heard that. I thought it might be a rumor."

"They're calling it the trial of the century. Not bad for a first run, Paige."

He gets up to leave.

"By the way . . . I knew you wouldn't kill him."

"Yeah, right."

He leans in and whispers, "In fact, why do you think I found you?" He stands up straight. "The world needs to question the dominant paradigm."

He gives me a kind of secret, knowing look and walks off.

Halfway out the door he turns around.

"Oh, I left something for you."

He nods and walks into the gluten-free, iced chai distance.

And there it is. Under the table. Something framed.

I open the brown crepe paper, indistinct, and look inside.

There it is, that coyote painting from the dirtbag flea motel, howling at the moon. The one I said I wanted to buy ironically. In Monument Valley.

I can't believe he got this for me. But more than that, I can't believe there is something taped to the back of it.

Ah.

I see.

My next mission.

ACKNOWLEDGMENTS

I wonder if I will forget someone? If I do, please forgive me. I have been helped in so many ways, by so many people, I am both in awe and gratitude.

So, here goes: my mother, father, brother, sister, step-mom, and stepdad. To my agent, Rosemary Stimola, who is my cookies and milk. To my editor, Kristen Pettit, who has been incredible, kind, brilliant, and just plain cool. To Elizabeth Lynch and everyone over at HarperCollins, in those glassy rooms, with Herman Melville's contract somewhere on display. In LA, I must thank my agent, Jordan Bayer, at Original Artists. I have to thank Wyck Godfrey and Jaclyn Huntling over at Temple Hill. Your insight into this book, and the film, has been truly inspiring and essential. Of course, Greg Mooradian and everyone at Fox 2000. I must thank my close friends Dawn Cody, Brad Kluck, Mira Crisp, and Io Perry. You are such good eggs. And, of course, my husband, journalist and rabble rouser, Sandy Tolan. I love you with all my heart and, especially, the way you never fail to rattle the cages on behalf of those in need. You are truly my better half. And, last, but not least, my beloved son, Wyatt. I could shake out all the stars in the sky and never make as much light as you.

Don't miss these books by
ANDREA PORTES

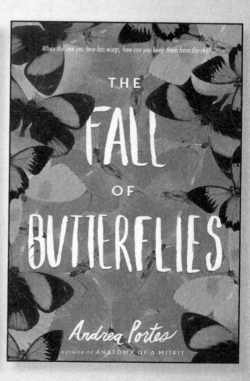

JOIN THE
Epic Reads
COMMUNITY

THE ULTIMATE YA DESTINATION

◄ DISCOVER ►
your next favorite read

◄ MEET ►
new authors to love

◄ WIN ►
free books

◄ SHARE ►
infographics, playlists, quizzes, and more

◄ WATCH ►
the latest videos

www.epicreads.com

SAN T POR